Catch Me If You Can

Liliana Hart

ISBN-10: **1470035006**

ISBN-13: **978-1470035006**

To Dallas-

Because you make me laugh

Also By Liliana Hart

Novels

Catch Me if You Can
Diagnosis: Love
Dirty Little Secrets
Paradise Disguised

Novellas

Cooper
Dane
Dominating Gracie
Double Jeopardy
Riley
The Madam Duchess
Thomas

CHAPTER ONE

The *slap, slap, slap* of his shoes hitting the pavement echoed in the fog that crept over the sleeping city.

He was slicked with sweat and his lungs burned with each laboring breath, but still he ran faster, punishing his body, punishing himself, as he fought the urge to look over his shoulder. It never seemed to matter how fast he ran, because his past continued to haunt him.

Shane Quincy knew all about ghosts and personal demons. He knew about the terror of the innocent and their screams that still filled his head. He knew about heartbreak and sorrow because it plagued him with every breath he took. And most of all, he knew about fear—fear that clawed its way up from the pit of his belly and left a bitter taste in his mouth—and horrors so devastating they could break even the toughest FBI Hostage and Rescue Sniper.

And he had been the toughest. The best the FBI had ever had to offer.

He slowed his steps as a heavy drizzle blanketed the deserted New Orleans street and hunched over, propping his hands on his knees as he gasped for breath and tried to ease the aching in his chest. He knew from experience that the ache would never go away, but he tried just the same.

For two years his routine hadn't changed. The nightmares would come, waking him in a cold sweat with the taste of bile rising in the back of his throat. The covers would be damp and twisted beneath his restless body and his senses would be primed. But the echoes of the screams were only in his imagination, so he'd slip on his sweatpants and a t-shirt, leave his empty apartment, careful not to disturb the dark-haired woman he shared the third floor with, and he'd run for miles through The Big Easy. Fast and hard, as if he were running for his life. And in some ways he was.

The drizzle turned into a downpour and Shane laughed bitterly as he raised his face to the sky. He began running again, this time at a slower tempo, and turned left off of First Street onto Prytania, where the historic mansion that housed six different apartment units was located. He never would have been able to afford the place when he was working for the FBI, but he'd found out very quickly after he'd turned in his resignation that private security paid a hell of a lot more than working for the government.

His skin was chilled and his dark hair, which was in desperate need of a trim, dripped into his eyes as he typed in the security code for the wrought iron gate that protected him and the other residents. Only four of the six units were currently occupied, the effects of Katrina and Rita still making people wary of putting down roots. There was a young couple on the first floor, both of them attorneys at a large firm, a tenured professor at Loyola on the second floor, and the woman who'd moved in a couple of months ago across the hall from him.

Shane wasn't afraid to admit that the new neighbor had given him a restless night or two after she'd first moved in. Apparently a peaches and cream complexion, raven hair and pale blue eyes were enough to jump-start his libido after a long hiatus. He hadn't wanted a woman in two years.

Not since Maggie had died.

But he wanted his new neighbor, and because of the fierce need that had caught him unawares, he did his damnedest to stay out of her way. He didn't know anything about her and it didn't look like things would ever be any different since she'd never gone out of her way to say more than a lukewarm hello. The same could be said about all the neighbors, which in his opinion made it the perfect place to live.

Along the outside of the building, freshly painted, white wooden stair cases led to each level of the house and split in different directions to each apartment door. Shane was almost to the third floor before he smelled the smoke. The rain and the wind had dampened the scent so it was barely recognizable, but it was there. He was sure of it.

He raced the rest of the way to the third floor and saw the licks of flame taunting him from the windows. The sight was hypnotic, the reds and oranges of the fire as it danced a path of destruction. The front door and one of the windows was open, feeding the inferno with much needed oxygen so it spread quickly through the rooms, up the thick drapes and onto the ceiling. Black smoke billowed out the open window and door, and he cursed himself for leaving his cell phone on his nightstand. He heard the fire alarms shrieking and hoped the other tenants made it out safely.

He didn't pay attention to the splintered wood on the open door as he charged into the smoke and biting flames to see if his neighbor was still inside. His adrenaline was pumping and he didn't miss the irony of the situation, that a failure such as himself would be put in the role of hero once again. He hadn't been able to save anyone in a long time. He could barely save himself.

The apartment was a mirror image of his own, and he ran with familiarity down the long hallway to the bedrooms at the back. Paint blistered on the walls. Black smoke blurred his vision and clogged his lungs, so he ducked down on his hands and knees and crawled the rest of the way to the bedroom. The fire wasn't contained to one area but seemed to be everywhere at once, racing toward some unseen finish line where the prize was utter destruction. The blaze was scorching hot and windows shattered as the pressure built hotter and higher inside the fiery walls.

Shane heard the coughs and the pants that sounded more animal than human as he crawled over the threshold into the master bedroom. The air was slightly clearer, but it wouldn't be for long. He stood up quickly and used his shirt to wipe his burning eyes before taking stock of the situation. What he saw built a fury in his gut that he hadn't felt in a long time.

The woman was handcuffed to the wooden slats on her headboard, her eyes wide and panic-stricken, and they became even more so when she saw him enter the room. The lady was terrified, but not just of the fire. She was afraid of him, and her struggles became even more frantic. He knew she would have screamed if she could have, but the smoke was thick and she doubled over in a coughing fit. Her black hair was matted around her temples and the boxer shorts and tank top she'd been sleeping in were wilted and sweat slicked. Her wrist was raw and bloody where she'd been pulling against her restraints.

"I'm not going to hurt you," Shane called out. He didn't know if she heard him or not, but he moved toward her anyway because they were running out of time. He could hear the blare of sirens from below, but it was up to him to get them both out alive.

He touched her on the shoulder and was caught off guard as she came up swinging with her free hand. It barely glanced off his shoulder, but he was impressed by her tenacity. She was no coward, that was for sure.

"I'm not going to let you kill me!" she screamed. "When I get out of here I'm going to send you back to my uncle in a body cast."

She fought against him like a caged animal until he wrapped both of his arms around her and squeezed tightly.

"I'm not going to hurt you," he repeated. "We've got to get out of here. We're running out of time."

She went into another fit of coughing and he used her distraction to kick at the wooden slats on the headboard. They were sturdy and thick, the antique obviously made to last centuries. Shane kicked again and put everything he had behind the force. The woman finally caught on that he was there to help and began pulling her weight against the steel bonds. A crack echoed through the room as the headboard gave way, and Shane barely caught her as the momentum from pulling against the cuffs almost sent them both to the floor.

Shane grabbed her around the waist and hauled her up over his shoulder. The smoke from the hallway was billowing into the room, so he carried her into the bathroom and shut the door behind him, buying them a few precious seconds. The large picture window behind the tub was the only way out. Black smoke crept under the door, and Shane used the small vanity chair sitting at the woman's dressing table to knock out the glass in the window. Fresh oxygen whooshed into the room and he gulped in a breath before the smoke found the opening he'd made.

He looked down three stories and felt his heart lodge in his throat. He'd been in a lot of deadly situations and thought he was going to die on more than one occasion, but he couldn't remember the feeling ever being more prevalent than it was right now.

They couldn't jump three stories. It was out of the question.

The bathroom window overlooked the side of the house, and if he leaned out far enough he could see the wide, wrap-a-round porch that led to their front doors. Black smoke still billowed out the front door and open windows, but the fire department was at work, taming the beast as best they could with gallons of water. If he could throw her far enough and then jump himself, they might just have a chance. It was their only option.

Shane put the woman down gently and noticed her eyes were still wide with shock. He stripped his shirt off and used it to clear the glass shards from the window so he didn't cut them both to pieces.

"Are you with me, Sugar?" he asked, swiping his thumb across her sooty face. "I'm going to toss you over to the railing. Do you think you're strong enough to grab hold?"

"I'm strong enough," she said with assurance. "And I'm not your Sugar."

"Yes, maam," Shane said with a smile and grabbed her around the waist. He maneuvered them both out the window until he straddled the sill. "Use your feet to propel you," he instructed as he showed her where to place her feet.

"On three," he said.

He waited for her nod and began to count. "One, two..."

Shane heaved with all his might at the same time that she pushed off the windowsill. Time was suspended as she flew through the air. He could hear every heartbeat that thudded in his chest and waited, what seemed like minutes but in reality was only a few short seconds, until she caught the railing with both hands.

He took a split second to heave a sigh of relief and then went after her, propelling himself off the ledge with a strength that had been lying dormant for two years. He climbed over the railing quickly and helped pull her over before grabbing her around the waist and hurtling down the stairs as fast as his legs could carry both of them.

Shane noticed the other tenants standing back away from the house in their nightclothes. They were unharmed and stood transfixed as the wild orange fire was conquered. The cop in him looked around to see if anyone was overly interested in the blaze, but there was no one that stood out in the crowd. He noticed the woman was doing the same, but she was fading fast into exhaustion and shock. If someone wanted to kill her, she would be an easy target after the ordeal she'd just gone through.

The EMT's met them both with oxygen, and a cop unlocked the cuff around the woman's wrist. Shane could tell the officer wanted to ask questions, but the woman went into another fit of coughing and he backed off so the medics could do their job. Shane stayed as close to her as he dared and kept his eyes moving over the faces in the crowd. The lady had some explaining to do, and he wasn't going to let her out of his sight until she answered his questions.

The medics tended to her wrist, wrapping it in gauze and tape, and then left the two of them sitting in the back of an ambulance. Shane took the oxygen mask off his face and turned to look at her. Despite what they'd been through, she was still beautiful. Her eyes were the pale blue of an Alaskan Husky and they looked at him with weariness and distrust.

"I'm Shane Quincy," he said, extending his hand. "I live across the hall from you."

She looked at his hand like it was poisonous, but she eventually took it. "Yes, I recognize you now. It was hard to see with all the smoke."

Her voice was husky and pure lust tingled along his spine with each word that was spoken. The combination of the adrenaline rush and not being with a woman for so long was playing havoc with his senses.

"I guess I should thank you for saving my life," she said.

"I'd settle for your name." Shane could tell she was thinking about lying to him.

"Rachel."

"Do you have a last name, Rachel?"

"Just Rachel will do," she said firmly.

"Well, just Rachel, do you want to tell me who the hell your uncle is and why he sent someone to murder you?"

Jimmy Grabbaldi knew his plan was going to fail as soon as he saw the jogger start up the stairs to his third floor apartment. Who the hell jogged in the middle of the night, anyway?

But he decided to stay and watch the scene play out. It wouldn't bother him any if there were two casualties instead of one. As long as the job got done. That's what was important.

He'd watched the big white mansion from dawn till dusk for two weeks, easily passing as a tourist with a camera on the busy street in the Garden District, snapping pictures of the tenants and their patterns. The park across the street had provided cover. There were plenty of secluded areas hidden by magnificent trees and large shrubs. He'd put on his tackiest Hawaiian shirt and cargo shorts and brought a book and a sack lunch each day, setting up the scene on one of the park benches that had a perfect view of the mansion. No one bothered him, and no one saw him taking closer looks with the binoculars he kept in his bag. He'd finally felt it was time to make his move and get back to Chicago.

He'd passed the evening at Pat O'Brien's Bar down in the French Quarter, nursing a couple of glasses of Irish Whiskey and charming a waitress named Candy into inviting him over to her place after she was through with her shift. Jimmy never thought of himself as an attractive man. He skimmed just under six feet and had the body of a brawler and the crooked nose to prove it was true. His hair was dark, his eyes small and black and his complexion bad, but he never had trouble scoring with the ladies. The one thing he did have going for him was that he looked dangerous, and that was its own attraction to a certain kind of woman. Apparently Candy fell into that group.

He'd left Pat O'Brien's just after three o'clock with a soft buzz and Candy's address in his pocket. He didn't have anything with him, no I.D. or wallet, just a money clip with a couple thousand in cash for business expenses. He took his time and walked almost three miles from the French Quarter to Prytania Street in the Garden District. Jimmy had always found it was to his advantage to do his crimes while it was raining because the cops didn't like to leave their dry cars to check out anything suspicious. He'd left his car on a crowded side street adjacent to Rachel's apartment so he could get away quickly if things went wrong, but things hardly ever went wrong when he set out to do a job.

No one saw him enter the park across the street from the big white mansion, or move aside the branches from his hiding place to uncover a cardboard packing box. It held everything he needed: A milk jug of kerosene, matches, old rags he'd made from clothes he'd gotten at the Salvation Army, a pen light, a crowbar and finally the handcuffs.

He'd thought out everything to the exact detail. That's what the boss paid him for, and he was very successful at his job. They didn't call him "The Grim Reaper" for nothing. He knew the code to the gate. The binoculars had picked it up easily, and none of the tenants except the guy on the third floor had bothered to cover the numbers. He'd carried the box and its contents up the three flights of stairs, sweating slightly and huffing a bit by the time he reached the top.

It was black as pitch, so he had to pick at the thick tape that held the box closed by feel. When the box finally opened, he dug around for the penlight and stuck it between his teeth before getting out the crowbar. The door was sturdy, but the locks were flimsy and it was just the break he needed. The door splintered open and he was inside in just a few seconds. He immediately began dousing the rags and laying them around the apartment to make a trail to the front door. He poured the rest of the gasoline on the rugs and curtains and dumped the cardboard box in the middle of the living room before heading back to the bedroom.

She was lying on her stomach, and a long expanse of pale leg was visible from where he stood. She'd left the bathroom light on, so he put the pen light in his pocket and pulled out the cuffs. He could see the curtain of her dark hair as it framed her face, and her breathing was slow and easy. It was a shame the boss wanted to knock her off. A waste of a good woman in his opinion. But the boss had his reasons—the most important being that Rachel Valentine was a threat.

The quiet click of the cuffs being fastened to her wrist and then to the headboard didn't wake her—the empty bottle of wine sitting next to a thick novel and a pair of reading glasses on the nightstand had helped him out in that regard. Jimmy figured he'd let her sleep through her death. It was the least he could do for Dom's daughter. Kind of a last tribute.

He struck a match as he walked back out the front door and dropped it onto the soaked rags. They didn't flare and spread as quickly as he would have liked, but it would get the job done. He left the door open and started back down the stairs, looking for any potential witnesses.

He saw the jogger once he got to the bottom of the stairs and immediately took cover behind the garbage bins. The guy was huge, and Jimmy didn't want to risk any type of involvement because he had a feeling he'd come out the loser. The man was at least 6'4" and muscled. If the guy had been at Pat O'Brien's, Jimmy had no doubt who Candy would have given her address to.

So when the man charged ahead into the smoke and flames and through Rachel's front door, Jimmy took the opportunity to sneak back across the street to the park and watch the action from a distance. And when Rachel and the guy both came out together, Jimmy knew he'd failed. The boss wasn't going to be happy with this latest setback. His orders had been to get rid of Rachel Valentine and get the hell out of New Orleans, and Angelo Valentine wasn't one to give second chances very often. Jimmy was dreading the phone call he was going to have to make.

On second thought, maybe he wouldn't place the call just yet. He could follow her and take care of the problem in the next couple of days. He'd be back in Chicago before the weekend.

CHAPTER TWO

Shane waited patiently for Rachel's answer and knew whatever it was wouldn't be good.

"I don't know what you're talking about," she answered, taking off her own oxygen mask and hopping down from the back of the ambulance. The medics had given each of them a thin plastic poncho to keep the rain off, but it wasn't enough to ward off the October chill.

"Well, Sugar, let me see if I can jog your memory," Shane said, frustrated. "Someone broke into your apartment tonight, cuffed you to the bed and set the place on fire. I don't know where you come from, but down here that's considered attempted murder."

Her glare could have cut glass, it was so penetrating. She tried to walk away but changed her mind when she saw the officer headed in her direction. "Just leave me alone. I've got to get out of here. Everything I owned was in that apartment and now it's all gone."

"Which is just part of the reason you're going to need my help."

"I don't want or need your help. I'm perfectly capable of taking care of myself."

"Obviously. You did a bang up job at hiding from whoever is trying to kill you. Why don't you tell me about your uncle?" he asked, trying to keep her off guard.

She jerked around suddenly, her nerves showing for the first time that night. "I don't have an uncle."

"Don't lie to me, sweetheart. Near death is not the time most people feel like making up stories. You said very clearly that your uncle was trying to kill you. The cop that's headed in your direction is going to want some answers, and I could make things pretty difficult for you. He's going to want to know who did this."

"It's not his problem, or yours," she said, unknowingly moving closer to his side when the cop approached. "I just want to get away from here."

Shane wanted to smile. He had her right where he wanted her. Subconsciously she already trusted him, even though her brain was probably telling her she couldn't trust anyone.

With good reason, he thought.

He put his arm around her and felt the tremors from adrenaline overload and the cold she'd been trying to contain unsuccessfully. Shane didn't recognize the cop. Through his business he'd run into most of them at one time or another, and most of them knew Shane by reputation.

"I need to ask you a few questions, ma'am," the officer said when he finally made it over to them. His uniform was pressed and starched severely, the rain hitting the surface and then sliding off the fabric in big fat drops. The stiffness could be nothing but uncomfortable against his considerable bulk. The night air was cool, and the stinging rain made it even colder. Shane was only wearing his sweatpants and running shoes and Rachel the thin cotton boxers and t-shirt she'd slept in. She didn't even have shoes.

Shane pulled her closer and she burrowed into his warmth. His body temperature spiked suddenly at the feel of her pressed against him. His body was a raging inferno, and he was surprised the rain didn't sizzle off his sensitized skin. He'd never understand why hormones always picked the most inopportune times to want attention.

Shane looked at the officer's name plate and made a decision, whether Rachel would go along with it time would only tell.

"Officer Broussard, we've both had a really difficult night." An uncontrollable shiver chose that moment to wrack Rachel's body, and Shane was pretty sure she wasn't that good of an actress. At least he hoped she wasn't. The shiver did the trick though because Broussard's hard eyes softened and he looked at her with pity. "All she has left are the clothes she's wearing. She doesn't even have shoes. Is there any way we can come into the station tomorrow to answer your questions?"

Officer Broussard looked both of them over and then made his decision. "First thing in the morning," he said stiffly. "This was no accident, and the longer we wait the less likely we are to catch whoever did this." He walked away and got into his cruiser, watching the firemen put out the last of the flames from the warmth of the car.

"Listen," Rachel said, pulling away from him. "I really appreciate your help. I wouldn't be here if it wasn't for you, but you don't understand what you're dealing with. I have to get out of here, and I have to do it alone. They'll kill you too if you're with me."

Shane was glad she was finally starting to give him a little honesty. "I don't think you know who you're dealing with, Sugar. But this isn't just about you anymore. Whoever did this could have killed everyone in the building tonight. Me included. I can take care of myself, and I can track down who's responsible a hell of a lot faster than Officer Friendly over there."

She was shaking her head and looked ready to run as far away from him and New Orleans as possible. "I can't ask you to do that," she pleaded.

"You don't have to. Besides, this is our very first date. It'll be a hell of a story to tell our grandkids. I'm not quite ready to let you get away now that I've met you and put a name to that stunning face."

"You're out of your mind."

Shane didn't acknowledge her statement. Maybe he was out of his mind. He wasn't one to act on impulse. Not ever. He'd been trained to think out scenarios for every situation. He didn't even know what this situation was yet, but it didn't matter because his priority had become keeping Rachel alive.

"Let's get out of here," he said, taking her by the arm and leading her over to a large black Tahoe. "I've got some things to pick up at my office."

"I don't even know you," she protested.

"That's all right, Sugar. I have a feeling we're going to get to know each other real well before this is over." He gave her a look hot enough to make her blush and put his Tahoe in reverse, speeding away from the flashing lights and the dwindling crowd toward the Central Business District. Neither of them noticed Jimmy Grabbaldi watching from his hiding place across the street.

Commuter traffic was just getting started as they made their way down the rain-slicked streets toward Shane's office. There was still another hour of dark, and the rain had turned back into a miserable drizzle.

"What is it exactly that you do?" Rachel finally asked after several minutes of uncomfortable silence. She'd spent the short car trip with her arms folded across her chest and her eyes staring straight ahead, but she was all too aware of the man sitting beside her.

"I work in private security," he finally answered.

"Is that like a private detective?"

"It's whatever the client wants. Sometimes it involves bodyguard work, and sometimes it involves tracking down people who don't want to be found."

"How long have you been doing it?"

"What is this, a job interview?" Shane asked. "I told you I was qualified to help you with whatever your problems are. I can probably even dig up a few references if it makes you feel better."

The "mind your own business" signal couldn't have been stronger if he'd been wearing a sign, but Rachel had never been one to give up easily. If she had, she'd already be dead.

"I have a right to know who you are. You've

shanghaied my life and not given me any choice in the matter. Of course, I can always walk away just as soon as you stop the car. No harm, no foul."

The threat was made, but Rachel didn't want to walk away. She was tired of running, tired of hiding, and tired of looking over her shoulder every time she went to the grocery store. She needed help. And fate had stepped in and given her a bodyguard for a neighbor.

"You look like a cop. But more," she said, eyeing him carefully now. She'd gotten plenty of looks at him in the two months she'd lived to New Orleans. She'd have to be dead not to notice the dark-eyed god who lived across the hall. He looked like a fallen angel. His hair was dark and longer than she usually preferred on a man, hanging just past his ears and over his collar. His skin was swarthy, and his eyes were so black that the pupil and iris couldn't be differentiated. She'd lay awake at night and listen to him run his fingers over the piano in his apartment, playing bluesy numbers, and imagine what those same fingers would feel like touching her.

"I was a Marine sniper during the Gulf War, and then I did more of the same for the FBI Hostage and Rescue Unit," he answered quietly.

Rachel flushed because she'd been staring at him so intently she'd forgotten what question she'd asked. Now was definitely not the time to be having inappropriate thoughts about a man she didn't even know. She looked at the hard set of his jaw and the white-knuckled grip he had on the steering wheel and knew it had cost him a lot to tell her that much about himself. She decided not to press the issue for now.

They turned on Tchoupitoulas Street and parked in front of a non-descript, beige, two-story building smashed between more of the same on either side. All the buildings had red awnings that hung over the sidewalk. Discreet gold letters painted on the window said, *Quincy Security and Investigations.*

"This is a lot bigger than I thought it would be," Rachel said.

"What, you were expecting some hole in the wall in the slums?"

"No, not exactly." But she hadn't thought it would be an operation as large as this. Shane Quincy must be very good at his job.

"I've got twelve men and women on staff full-time. All of them are retired law enforcement of some kind."

Rachel let him usher her into a small waiting area where a receptionist's desk and large fish tank sat among cool shades of gray and blue. She watched as he locked the door behind them and headed up carpeted stairs.

"I've got a small apartment up here that I use when I'm working late. It's got some extra clothes.

Unfortunately, I don't think my shoes are going to fit you."

"That's okay. I don't think your clothes are going to fit me either."

He laughed and the sound sent tingles down her spine. This was a dangerous man. He threw her a pair of dark gray sweats and white athletic socks and pointed her to a small bathroom.

"Go get dressed and then you need to start talking," he ordered. "I need to know what we're up against."

Rachel did as she was told without argument because he'd said the magic word. We. She no longer had to face her fears alone. And maybe by the time it was all over, her father could finally rest in peace.

Shane took off his sopping clothes and threw them in a basket by the bathroom door. He pulled on worn jeans, a white shirt and a flannel, and he exchanged his wet Nikes for a pair of dry ones.

He went over to the window and pulled down a slat on the blinds, peering out into the street below. It was just after six in the morning and the traffic was light. There wouldn't be anyone in the office for another couple of hours, but he planned to be long gone by then.

He sent his secretary an email letting her know he'd be out of the office for a few days on a case and to turn over any pressing matters to his second-in-command. Then he went to his safe and pulled out a stack of extra cash, two Glock .9mm's and a snub-nosed revolver to go in his ankle holster. He had plenty of ammunition. He put all of it into a black bag and went to a locked cabinet behind his desk. No matter how many handguns he owned, his true love was still a rifle.

He unlocked the cabinet and had just pulled out the M40 when he heard movement behind him. Rachel was silhouetted in the door, a halo of light shining behind her, with his sweatpants rolled up at the bottom and the sweatshirt hanging down to her knees.

His eyes roamed over her lazily, taking in her flushed cheeks and damp hair, and his body did a slow melt down. He put the M40 down carefully on his desk and started towards her.

"I thought you wanted to hear about who's trying to kill me," Rachel said.

Shane stopped a few paces in front of her. "I do," he said.

"If you keep looking at me like that you might never get to hear it. I need to leave the area as soon as possible."

Shane sighed and tried to reel his body back in.

She was right, but boy was it tempting to scoop her up and head to Mexico so they could make love in a cabana by the ocean for the next fifty years. He was about to suggest just that when she started to talk.

"My name is Rachel Valentine," she said quietly, her eyes willing him to understand.

Shane knew the name was familiar, but he couldn't remember why.

"My father was Dominic Valentine."

His eyes grew big at that bit of information and he muttered a short expletive.

"I see you've heard of him," she said with a forced laugh.

If she knew how well he'd known the Valentine brothers she would have run screaming for the door. Shane had spent so much time trying to ignore her since she moved in that he hadn't studied her features as carefully as he otherwise might have. But he recognized Rachel for who she was now. She'd only been about twenty the last time he'd seen her—her hair had been lighter, streaked with blonde as if she'd just spent a few weeks on a tropical island somewhere. He'd been a rookie at the FBI then, and his first assignment had been the infamous mob family. It would probably be best if Rachel never knew how close Shane had come to killing her father.

He watched as she closed her eyes and tried to

gather her composure. The woman was in big, big trouble. Dominic Valentine had been the head of the largest crime family still operating in the United States. They were based in Chicago, and Shane remembered reading that "Dom" as he was called by everyone, had gone missing just before he was supposed to testify in federal court.

"Why don't we sit down," Shane said, taking Rachel by the elbow and leading her over to a small loveseat. "Take your time. Do you need some water?"

She hiccupped out a small laugh and shook her head. "No, I'm fine. I'm tougher than I look."

He imagined she'd have to be to grow up in the Valentine family.

"I'm going to give you the short version, because I really need to get out of here. I feel like I've got a target on my forehead, and the itch at the back of my neck has been getting worse since we left the house."

"Just give me enough to know what I'm dealing with," Shane said.

"My father was ready to get out of the business. He hadn't been the same since my mother was killed several years ago, and things got worse after my younger sister was killed last year."

Shane remembered reading those bits of

information in the newspaper and thinking that crime, most definitely, did not pay. Both of the Valentine women had been taken out with very sophisticated car bombs.

"I'm sorry," he told her softly.

"He made the decision because of me. Because I was all he had left," she said. "I know in my brain that my father was a criminal. He did bad things. Things that I will never be able to justify. But he was a good father, and for that he deserves my love and devotion as a daughter."

"Nobody could fault you for loving your father," Shane said.

"No, but I'm what you might think of as collateral damage. When I say my father wanted out of the business to keep me safe, I mean that he wanted all the way out. And if he had to do time in federal prison because of his crimes he said it was worth it to keep me alive.

"He met with an agent named Donald Culver and agreed to confess to all of his financial transgressions and compile a list of all active mafia and their crimes if he and I could both be put in Witness Protection. You should have seen his face when he told me he was finished. He was so relieved. I didn't realize how old he'd gotten until that moment."

Shane let out a low whistle between his teeth.

"That would be one hell of a list for someone who's been around as long as Dom."

"Yes, but after dad met with Agent Culver at the Federal Building in Chicago and turned over the list, he went missing."

"When was the last time you spoke with him?"

"We spoke on the phone just after noon on the day he disappeared. He was scheduled to appear at the courthouse for a deposition and to meet with the district attorney. He knew they were going to arrest him, but he didn't seem to care."

"What happened to the list after your father disappeared?"

"Agent Culver was found with his throat slashed floating in Lake Michigan. The list hasn't been seen since, and no other agents will even admit to having seen it."

"They'd be signing their death warrants." Shane thought about everything Rachel had told him so far, processing bits of information, storing and discarding as needed. "So why are they after you, Rachel?" Shane finally asked, coming around to the one thing that didn't make sense.

"Because my father made a mistake."

"What mistake?"

"My father was blind when it came to his brother.

He believed all families should be loyal to each other, no matter the circumstance, but Uncle Angelo was never loyal to anyone but himself. Dad asked Angelo to protect me if anything should happen to him, and Angelo played him until he got the information he wanted.

"What information?"

"Dad told Uncle Angelo that he'd sent me a copy of the list for safe-keeping."

Shane shook his head in disbelief. "You have the copy of the list?" he asked incredulously. The fact that Rachel was still alive was a testament to her own abilities.

Stark pain came into Rachel's eyes. "Yes. It's in a safety-deposit box in Chicago. This is the reason I know Angelo killed my father. Because if dad were still alive I would have heard from him by now. Angelo wants the list, and he'll do everything he can to get it in his hands. I'm running out of places to hide where his men can't find me."

Shane thought of the tangles this particular situation would bring them. The worst-case scenario was that Angelo would torture them both before disposing of their bodies. The Valentine organization ran far and wide, and there would be few people along the way who could be trusted to keep them safe.

"So what do you say, Mr. Private Investigator?

Am I too dangerous for you?"

CHAPTER THREE

“I guess it’s lucky for you I like dangerous women,” Shane said after a minute of stunned silence. “We need to get out of here. You can tell me the rest on the way. You must be one hell of an amazing woman to have dodged them for this long.”

“You don’t grow up in the Valentine household without learning a few helpful tips, but I’ve felt Angelo’s men breathing down my neck over the last couple of months.”

Shane zipped up the black bag with the weapons, money and a few other necessities and slung it over his shoulder. He turned off the lights so only the glow from the computer screen was visible. He grabbed Rachel by the hand and pulled her toward him. She barely came up to his shoulder in her socked feet.

"I have to say I'm not terribly sorry for meeting you under circumstances such as these."

Her eyes were luminescent in the shadowed room, and he put his hand on the back of her neck and brought her closer. Her eyes fluttered closed as his lips hovered a breath away from hers. He recognized the low pull in his gut as her body fit against him. He was prepared to explore—her taste and texture—prepared to savor the soft sighs that would follow. But as he brushed his lips gently against hers, he realized he'd made a mistake. He wasn't prepared at all. Her mouth was a banquet, her lips sweet and her sighs intoxicating. He could lose himself in her taste alone.

He pulled away, knowing that if he kissed her again there would be no turning back. The part of himself he'd kept rigidly locked away would take over all rational thought, and it could only end in pain for them both because he would never be capable of giving what a woman like Rachel Valentine deserved.

But Rachel surprised him when she wouldn't let him back away. She wrapped her hands around the back of his neck and pulled him closer.

"Mmm, again," she moaned.

He knew it was a bad idea, but his brain was being overruled by more basic needs. He captured her mouth in a scorching kiss that held two years of pent up desire and longing. It was a kiss meant to stir passions, a kiss meant to threaten his control. It was carnal in its intensity as lips and tongues clashed.

He swallowed her moan and pulled her closer, so the heat of their bodies met and melded. He hadn't realized he'd been starved for the taste of a woman. But not just any woman. Only this one. Her hands fisted in his hair and he moved her backward, never lifting his lips from hers, until her legs hit the back of the small loveseat and they went down together in a heap of tangled limbs. His hand found its way beneath her shirt and his fingers grazed over a rigid nipple. She arched against him and he buried his face against her neck and fought for control.

What was wrong with him? He wondered. He had to get a grip, and fast.

No sooner had the thought entered his mind than the windows facing the street exploded and a boom echoed where only seconds before the room had been filled with sounds of passion. Terror and adrenaline replaced the feeling in an instant, and Shane rolled off the couch and tucked Rachel beneath him. The rapid-fire sounds of bullets hitting the building continued as they belly crawled to the stairwell.

"Sounds like he's got an HK MP5," Shane said, his voice calm and low.

"What's that?"

"Submachine gun. He'll have to stop and reload in a minute. When he does we need to get to the back door. There's an alleyway behind us."

"Gotcha," she said.

He admired the fact she hadn't lost control at the first sound of gunfire. They hunkered down again as the shots continued. The bottom windows were being taken care of now.

"I never realized I had so many windows," Shane said. "My secretary is going to be pissed."

"Do you think he followed us when we left the apartments?" Rachel asked. "I looked around, but I didn't see anyone who looked suspicious."

"Yeah, I did too, but there was plenty of cover to be found in the park across the street."

The gunfire stopped as suddenly as it had started and the silence left in its wake pulsed along with the pounding beats of their hearts.

"Let's go," Shane said. He grabbed the black bag and shoved Rachel in front of him, shielding her body with his own, as he pushed her down the stairs and led her through a long corridor of offices to an oversized steel door. The door opened soundlessly on well-oiled hinges, and cold rain beat against their skin as they ran into a dark alleyway.

“What are we going to do?” Rachel asked.

“We’ve got to find an alternate mode of transportation. There’s no way we can make it to the Tahoe without him seeing us.” Shane looked around the alley and noticed an older model Toyota. The paint had peeled in several places, the fender was rusted and the tires were bald. He didn’t think the car would get them down the street, much less to Chicago.

“What about that?” Rachel asked, pointing to a black and chrome Harley parked a ways down the alley behind the corner bakery.

“My kind of woman,” Shane said with a quick smile as he grabbed her hand and ran the rest of the way down the alley. He could only pray that the guy shooting out front wasn’t smart enough to think about checking the back entrances, but chances were if this guy worked for the Valentine family then he was plenty smart.

Rachel straddled the bike behind him and her arms wrapped loosely around his waist. Seconds ticked away in his head as he touched wires together and heard the sweet purr of the engine as it started and echoed through the quiet. They wouldn’t be able to keep the bike for long before it was reported stolen. It belonged to the tattooed bakery owner, and he’d notice it was missing as soon as he brought the first load of morning trash to the dumpsters.

"Do you know how to fire a gun?" Shane asked, giving Rachel a quick look over his shoulder as he held out the Glock.

"Point and shoot, right?" she answered with a smile that Shane couldn't interpret the meaning of.

"Just do the best you can." He revved the engine and shot out of the alley at a high rate of speed, studying every spot on the street he would have used to hide if he was the one doing the shooting. He caught the reflection of steel as the street light glanced off a weapon pointed in their direction.

"Nine o'clock," he yelled to Rachel as shots rang out and pinged into a car barely a foot from his front tire. The streets were slick with rain, but his mind and hands stayed in control as he guided the bike across the pavement. He didn't even flinch as Rachel fired three rounds in close succession. All three hit the corner of the building their attacker was shooting from. It was a hell of a shot, no matter how you looked at it, and it reminded him he knew absolutely nothing about Rachel Valentine other than the fact she sent his body into overdrive and came from a dangerous family who'd obviously taught her how to shoot to kill.

Rachel held on for dear life as Shane tore out of New Orleans like a bat out of hell. The feel of freedom washed over her with every mile that separated her from her hunter and giddiness and adrenaline was its own euphoria.

It was just past sunrise when they stopped in a small town outside of the city. Houses were few and far between and trees were thick and covered with vines. The fishermen and trappers who worked the bayous were long since gone and others were still fast asleep.

"What are we doing here?" Rachel asked. "Do you think we should stop so soon?"

"We've got to change vehicles. I guarantee the bike has already been reported stolen. It's only a matter of time before we're spotted."

Shane gave her a funny look and she wondered if she had bugs in her teeth from the motorcycle ride.

"Where the hell'd you learn to shoot like that?"

"At my daddy's knee, of course," she answered with an attempt at the thick Cajun accent she'd heard so many people speak with since she'd been in Louisiana. "I shot for sport in college. Team captain."

"If you ever want a job, lady, give me a call. You're almost as good as I am."

"I'd be glad to accept a challenge. Anytime. Anywhere." Rachel couldn't believe how brazen she was being with someone she barely knew. She'd never been much of a flirt, and she'd never been promiscuous, but there was something about Shane Quincy that made her want to throw up her hands and say, "To hell with it." Despite her father's notoriety, she'd lived a pretty sheltered life. Boyfriends had been few and screened carefully. Her roommate from college had been hand picked, and every tenant in her apartment building had had a thorough background check.

"Be careful. I never back away from a challenge," he said softly.

The intensity and heat in his stare was enough to bring a blush to her cheeks, and she looked everywhere but at him with a newfound purpose. "It doesn't look like we have a lot to choose from."

"We don't need anything fancy. Just something that will get us part of the way to Chicago."

Rachel watched as Shane looked in the windows of a beat up pickup truck. It was parked at the mouth of a bayou next to an old wooden dock. "We don't need to go to Chicago. We need to go to Dallas."

"Wait. Rewind," Shane said as he looked up from his task of hotwiring the truck. "Why do we need to go to Dallas? I thought the list was in a safety deposit box in Chicago."

The truck started with a sputtering cough and Shane threw in his duffle bag and practically tossed her into the cab.

"Why are we taking this? It won't do us any good if we break down on the side of the highway."

"Listen to the purr of that engine, Sugar. People down here drive older cars but they keep them in top shape. It wouldn't do them any good to try and evacuate for a hurricane and not be able to get their cars started. And we're taking this particular truck because the owner is obviously busy checking his traps for the day. Trappers don't usually come in until the afternoon, so it should give us plenty of time to get a head start."

"Oh," Rachel said.

"Now tell me why we're going to Dallas when the copy of the list is in Chicago."

Rachel bristled a little at the demand, but kept her mouth shut. She'd never been one for taking orders. "I work at a large interior design firm in Chicago. Worked," she clarified. It had broken her heart to give up the job she'd fought so hard for. Sacrificed for. "Dad called me on my cell at the office that last day. I was busy with client meetings, so I didn't give him as much time as I should have. As I wish now I had. He was excited and told me everything was going to work out just fine, and that Uncle Angelo would take care of me if anything went wrong. Dad was scheduled to meet with Agent Culver like I told you, and then give his deposition. I wished him luck, told him I loved him and hung up. I didn't give it another thought until I was told he was missing."

Rachel's voice cracked on a sob, but she pulled herself together. She hated to show any weakness. Especially in front of a stranger. Valentines did not cry. Her father always told her their enemies would constantly look for vulnerabilities, chinks in their armor. So she'd stood dry-eyed next to her father at the funerals of her mother and sister, though she'd been dying on the inside. If she could hold it together then, she could sure as hell hold it together in front of Shane Quincy.

Rachel took a few minutes to gather her composure and was thankful Shane stayed silent. The rain had picked up and was coming down in blinding sheets, but Shane handled the truck smoothly, focused on the road ahead. She hadn't seen him lose that focus in any of the situations that had been thrown at them so far.

She spoke softer as she continued. "Just as I was packing my things away for the day a Fed-Ex package landed on my desk. Someone at the front desk had signed for it and sent it up. Since it was sent to me at work I figured it was work related and shoved it into my briefcase. I didn't give it another thought until I unlocked the front door of my apartment."

"Let me guess," Shane said. "Someone had searched your apartment."

“Searched is too kind a word for what they did. They violated every inch of every space. Drawers were upended and furniture had been slashed to ribbons. My desktop was smashed to pieces on the floor and my laptop was gone. I took one look at the mess, turned around and got out of there.”

“You’re lucky you didn’t run into the person responsible.”

“Believe me, I know. I found out later that night on the news that my doorman’s body had been found in the alley with multiple gunshot wounds.”

“What did you do?”

“I took a taxi to the South Side and stayed in a dirt cheap motel until the next morning. I didn’t sleep a wink that night and jumped at every sound. When I opened the package that had been sent to me, I knew I held the power to destroy a lot of people’s lives. I think my father knew he probably wouldn’t live to see all the wrongs made right, so it’s up to me now.”

“That’s a lot of pressure to put on someone you love,” Shane said skeptically.

“My father was a good man,” Rachel insisted vehemently. “He’d want me to do the right thing.”

“So why are you in Louisiana instead of testifying before a grand jury, and how do you know that your father told Angelo he gave you a copy of the list?”

This guy was a hard nut to crack. It was a good thing Rachel wasn't looking for sympathy, because she felt sure he didn't possess the emotion. Her voice frosted over and was hard as ice when she continued.

"Because the police discovered a message when they found my doorman's body in the alley. Angelo's men had carved a warning into the poor man's chest, demanding that I turn over the list or I'd be next. A news camera got it on film, and I saw the whole thing with the rest of the world on the ten o'clock news. The next morning I borrowed a car from the lot of the motel I was staying at and drove back to Chicago."

"When you say borrowed, I take it you mean stole."

"Are you going to let me finished the story or not?"

"By all means," he said.

"I was at my bank just as they were opening, and I told the clerk I needed to put some things in my safety deposit box. My father made sure I was prepared in case something like this happened, so I removed a duffle bag from the box similar to the one you carry. It was full of cash and ID's, an extra set of clothes and a couple of wigs. I made a copy of the papers and put the originals in the safety deposit box.

I changed clothes and hair in the restroom and walked out the front door without anyone noticing."

"I can put two and two together and assume you sent the copies of the papers you made to someone in Dallas. But that still doesn't answer my question. How are you supposed to turn this evidence over to the FBI if you're running away?"

Rachel looked at Shane and wondered not for the first time if she was getting more with him than she'd bargained for. She was out of people she could trust. The list had been short to begin with, but now most of them were dead, and she didn't want to involve her two closest friends in anything that could get them hurt. Trusting a stranger might be her best shot at survival. Or Shane Quincy could be working for her Uncle Angelo and kill her for the large price that had been put on her head. Her instincts were failing her, and for the first time she wondered if she could even trust herself.

Shane noticed the sudden fear in her eyes but stayed silent, quietly driving the stolen truck along rutted and muddy paths. They'd be in Texas before they hit a highway that wouldn't jar teeth or spew mud onto passing cars.

"You're not going to get rid of me so easy now," Shane said. "Whoever's after you could have burned down my house and they destroyed my business. I'm in this for the long haul, so you might as well stay on for the ride."

The quick show of fear she'd displayed disappeared. Shane felt her cool stare and the calculating gaze of her weighing the odds of putting her safety in his hands. He kept his grip relaxed over the steering wheel and waited for her to make up her mind.

"Fine, but I prefer to treat this as a business relationship."

His curse was short and obscene, but she wasn't rattled.

"Hear me out," she said. "I don't like being out of control, and I've never had much faith in my fellow man. In my world people don't just do things for others out of the goodness of their hearts. But money, honor and pride are always important. Especially in my family. So it makes sense to hire you and your agency to track down the list and protect me when I hand it over to the FBI. There's no reason I'd have to testify. I have no knowledge of any business dealings my father had going and don't care to. We'd have a binding contract until I feel I'm in no further danger. And if you do happen to be working for my Uncle Angelo, just know that what I plan to pay you for your services will be far more than anything he could ever dream to offer you. Uncle Angelo doesn't hold the strings to the Valentine bank accounts since my father's disappearance. I do."

Shane clenched his jaw and the throbbing pulse in his neck told him just how pissed off her proposal made him. He'd been through horrors she could never dream of, serving and protecting his country while watching his friends die. Did she think he knew nothing of honor? Of pride? But then he closed himself off to his anger and analyzed the real reason for being so upset, just as he'd been taught to do in the Marines. Yes, he was offended that Rachel didn't trust him more, but he could hardly blame her for that when he hadn't trusted anyone but himself in the last two years.

The problem was that he wanted her. All of her. He wanted to know everything about her. What made her tick and what made her laugh. And how her body would feel wrapped around his in the middle of the night. And if she paid him for his services, then his pride and honor would be at stake. Two things he'd never been able to compromise. Which meant that Rachel Valentine was off limits.

"Fine," he agreed. "But you'll have to be satisfied with a verbal agreement. Organization at my office is a little spotty right now."

CHAPTER FOUR

Rachel breathed easier for the rest of the trip into Dallas. She'd found comfort in Shane's anger. She needed a clear head now more than ever, and keeping Shane Quincy and his scorching kisses at arms length was exactly what she needed to get through this ordeal with a clear head and an unbroken heart.

The rain had disappeared as soon as they'd crossed the border into Texas, and the sun was shining brightly despite the briskness in the air. They'd stopped at Wal-Mart just before lunch, and Shane had run in and grabbed her some clothes and a pair of shoes. She'd changed in the cab of the truck while Shane had switched license plates with the car next to them.

"So where are we going to get the list?" he finally asked. "Did you send it to a friend down here?"

“No, I sent it to a lawyer who tried to prosecute Dad several years ago. I figured it would be safe in his hands. He’s stuck with client privilege since I pay him a retainer. I think it would be best for both of us if we could get the list without having to go to Chicago. Angelo has eyes and ears everywhere, and they’ll know the moment I step foot into the city.”

Shane knew she spoke the truth. The farther they could stay from Chicago, the safer they’d be. “It was a smart plan. Very smart,” Shane acknowledged. “I’ve got a couple of pay as you go cell phones in the bag. Grab one and give the man a call. Let him know we’re coming to see him.”

Rachel’s own cell phone was still back in her apartment, so she had to call directory assistance to get his number. She wished now she would have thought to grab it before Shane had thrown her out the window. It had all her important contact information in it.

She waited patiently for the operator to connect her to the law offices of Decker and Marsh. It was just after three o’clock in the afternoon, and she hoped she’d be able to catch him in his office.

“Decker and Marsh,” a perky receptionist answered. “How may I help you?”

“I need to speak with Galen Marsh. It’s urgent.”

“Mr. Marsh isn’t taking calls right now. Can I take a message?”

"This is Rachel Valentine. I believe Mr. Marsh will take time to speak with me." Rachel heard a rustle of papers over the line and a few whispered voices. It must have been a new girl in the office.

"Hold please," the perky voice said.

Easy listening music came over the line, and she waited less than a minute before her attorney answered the phone.

"Rachel," Galen Marsh said, his voice cracking. "Where have you been? I haven't heard from you in months."

Something was wrong. It was impossible to ignore the nervousness in his voice. Galen Marsh hadn't been thrilled when she'd "put him on her payroll" as he liked to call it. He never let an opportunity pass to remind her where she came from and that he thought no more of her than he had of her father. In Galen Marsh's eyes, anyone with the last name of Valentine should be locked behind bars. But it hadn't stopped him from taking her money. And despite his personal feelings about her family, she knew he wouldn't compromise his career by betraying her trust. It was just like she'd explained to Shane. Money talked, and there was such a thing as honor among thieves.

"What's going on, Galen?" Rachel asked, cutting right to the chase.

He sighed over the other end of the line, and she

could imagine him shifting his considerable bulk behind the polished wood of his antique desk and reclining back in his chair. No doubt if he could have lifted his feet from the floor to the desk, they'd be propped there.

"You've got quite a few of your people looking for you, Rachel," he finally said.

"What do you mean, my people?"

"Your family. They seemed worried about you. Wanted me to let them know where to find you."

"You didn't tell them, did you?" she asked, panic evident in her voice.

"Of course not. Anyway, it's not like you've been keeping me up to date where you've been hiding."

"What's the problem then, Galen? And keep the lawyer speak to a minimum. Just the truth in a hundred words or less."

"It's just that they somehow found out that you've hired me." His voice had turned whiny and it was everything Rachel could do not to cringe at the petulant tone in his voice.

"And that bothers you because if they were able to find out I'm a client, then others might be able to find out as well. Am I right?"

"It's true I'd have preferred to keep our business relationship quiet. It won't make my other clients feel too comfortable when they're told that known criminals keep me on the payroll."

Rachel's voice turned icy and she wished she could have reached through the phone to strangle the pompous man on the other end. "As far as I know, Mr. Marsh, your clients don't include any criminals, known or otherwise. Make sure you relay the message. Am I clear?"

"Sure, sure," he said. "I just don't want any trouble. Your relatives make quite a statement, and I've got a family to think about."

"Just do your job and keep telling them you don't know anything," Rachel said.

"I *don't* know anything. Maybe you feel like enlightening me."

Rachel softened her voice and tried her best to add a little charm, but sometimes even she couldn't work miracles. "If you play your cards right, Mr. Marsh, you're going to be one of the most famous attorneys in the United States. I can guarantee you that much."

He laughed indulgently. "And how do you plan to pull that off, Ms. Valentine? You're father's as good as dead, so there's not much of a chance for me to put him behind bars where he belongs."

Rachel gritted her teeth and held back all the vile thoughts that came to her mind every time her attorney opened his mouth. “No, but you might have heard my uncle is controlling certain areas of the business now.”

“Sure, but everyone knows it’s only a matter of time before he’s taken out. He doesn’t have the charisma that Dom had. Word is there’ve been a few problems on the inside.”

“Could be. I don’t keep up with the family business. I have bigger fish to fry. Like catching the bastards who took my father before he was able to testify.”

“Yeah, it’s a damn shame they couldn’t have gotten him after he spilled the information on all his rivals. It would have been a hell of a coup for the Justice Department. A victory all around.”

“Exactly,” Rachel said, hating the man more with every word that came out of his mouth. “I sent you a certified letter and a package several months ago with instructions to keep the package in a safe place and never open it. Do you have the package close by?”

“What’s in that package, Rachel?”

“Do you have it close by?” she repeated.

“Yeah, it’s in my office safe with all my own personal papers.”

“Good. I need that package today. We’re about

half an hour from your office. I'll swing by and get it."

"No, I don't want you coming here. There have been too many people asking about you lately. I've already told them I don't know anything, but I'd hate to think of what they'd do to me if they thought I'd been lying all this time. The office closes at five. Meet me in the parking garage across the street at five thirty. I'll bring the package as long as you promise to find another attorney when this is all over. I'm too close to retirement to have to worry about looking over my shoulder every time a Valentine comes in to town."

Rachel was silent for a few seconds. She wanted to demand he put the package in her hand now, but there was no reason not to wait and play things his way. She wasn't completely heartless, and she did understand his reasons for wanting to stay clear of her.

"Five-thirty, Mr. Marsh," she finally agreed. "And I'm sure I don't have to remind you not to tell anyone of our conversation."

Rachel hung up and turned in her seat to look at Shane. She hadn't even noticed he'd parked the truck in an abandoned parking lot just off the highway.

"I take it there's no love lost between you and your attorney," he said with a smile.

"You could say that." Rachel hadn't realized how

much tension had gathered in her shoulders once she'd heard the sound of Galen Marsh's voice. She slowly exhaled and stretched her sore muscles.

"He won't give us the package until office hours are over," she said to fill the empty silence as Shane's gaze never left her. The pulse at the base of her throat began to flutter and her palms started to sweat. The man made her more nervous than anyone she'd ever met, and considering some of the people she'd known in her lifetime, that was saying something.

"Well, I guess we'll have to find something to do to fill the time," he finally said.

Unfortunately, that's what she was afraid of.

What Rachel hadn't expected was a trip to the zoo.

"Excuse me, Mr. Hot Shot Investigator, but I was under the impression we were running for our lives. Not taking a vacation."

Shane pulled a black ball cap out of his bag and put it on, along with a pair of dark sunglasses. "Has anyone ever told you that you need to have a little faith sometimes?"

"No, and if you'd come from my family you wouldn't have faith in anyone or anything other than yourself either."

"Good point," he acknowledged. "I need to make a call to someone at the FBI and see if he has any information that could be of use to us. I need to know who to contact once we make it to Chicago. The zoo is always crowded, there are plenty of places to get lost if we need to, and do you see all of these towers surrounding us? They'll confuse the phone signal and give us a little extra time to get away if someone's listening in on my conversation."

"Do you think we lost the guy who shot at us in New Orleans?"

"I haven't noticed anyone tailing us, but it never hurts to be careful. I would never underestimate anyone who works for your family. They are professional and persistent."

"You seem to know a lot about my family."

Shane kept his face blank while wishing he could kick his own ass. It was in everyone's best interest for Rachel to never find out how well he knew the major players in her father's organization. "Everyone who has ever worked for the FBI knows something about your family," he hedged. He took her hand and led her into the zoo. "From what you told me about the conversation with your attorney, they could already have Marsh's phones tapped. Stay alert. If it is your uncle behind the attacks you might recognize someone."

"Doubtful. My father had more than two hundred employees, but I would bet that my Uncle Angelo has moved his own men up in the ranks. Just to ensure loyalty. It's what I would do."

They found a shaded spot near the elephants that was relatively quiet, and Shane pulled out one of the disposable cell phones. He dialed a number that had a few too many digits and waited as he was connected to Washington, D.C.

"I need to speak with Director Boyle. Tell him Shane Quincy is on the line."

"So the prodigal son returns," Harlan Boyle said after a few minutes. His voice was dark and rich like expensive chocolate, and a hint of the south still lingered no matter how hard he tried to get rid of it. "I knew you'd come back, boy. A man like you isn't meant to sit behind a desk."

Shane felt comfort in his old supervisor's words because he knew they were sincere. It hadn't been Harlan Boyle's fault that Shane's last job had turned into his own personal hell. Harlan Boyle had only been Deputy Director at the time. "Sorry to disappoint you, sir, but the desk suits me well."

"Doubtful, but I'll let you have your illusions. To what do I owe the honor of this phone call?"

"I have information on the Dominic Valentine situation. I need to know who the contact is in the Chicago office."

Director Boyle let out a low whistle. “That’s a pie you don’t want to stick your fingers in, son. People have a tendency to disappear when they know too much about the Valentines.”

Shane glanced and Rachel out of the corner of his eye. Her dark head was tilted back against a shade tree, her eyes were closed and her breathing was slow and even. He would have thought she was asleep except for the way her hands were clamped together in a white-knuckled grip.

“I know, sir. But sometimes you just have to do what’s right. I’ve got information that could potentially save a lot of people and a witness I’m trying to protect. There are very few people I can trust right now.”

“I guess I should be flattered I’m on the short list,” Harlan said. “But I’d prefer you not tell anyone you got the information from me. Director Shaw runs the Chicago office, and Special Agent Culver was one of his men. Shaw wasn’t too happy to find Culver practically decapitated and fed to the fishes, and he’s lost two other agents since then. You can imagine why no one works too hard to find where Dominic Valentine and his infamous list ended up.”
“You think there’s a leak on the inside?”

“They haven’t found any evidence to prove it, and believe me, they’ve looked. I believe the agent who headed up the internal investigation is a buddy of yours. Jones Daugherty.”

"You're kidding me? He's working IA?" Shane was speechless. Jones "Wildcat" Daugherty had been the team leader of the Alpha Squadron, a unit of seven men specialized in taking down terrorists. The Alpha Squadron had done two tours in Iraq together, but Shane had lost touch with everyone he'd served with after he'd left the FBI. The last he'd heard, Wildcat was climbing up the military career ladder.

"I can't see Wildcat Daugherty working for the FBI. Talk about someone who shouldn't be sitting behind a desk."

"Word around the Bureau is that he's damned good at it," Harlan said. "He's cleaned up a lot of messes in just a few months, but the Valentine situation isn't one of them."

"Thanks for the information, sir. I owe you one."

"I've got a job here for you whenever you're ready to come back."

"I don't owe you that much," Shane said with a laugh and hung up.

"Did you get the information you needed?" Rachel asked.

"Some of it. I don't want to make contact with the Chicago office until we're on the move again." Shane stood and stretched his muscles. He grabbed Rachel by the hand and pulled her into his arms, rubbing the knotted muscles at her shoulders.

"I don't mean to tell you how to do your job," she said, "but there's a man in a hat over there who seems awfully interested in us."

Shane pulled her closer so it looked as if they were embracing and whispered in her ear. "Yeah, it took him about five minutes to find us after I called my old headquarters."

"I thought the towers were supposed to give us a little time."

"Theoretically. But I know for sure now that Angelo has a plant inside the FBI. There's no other way they could have tracked us that fast otherwise."

"What are we going to do?" Rachel asked.

Shane took advantage of their situation by nipping lightly at her ear. She sucked in an unsteady breath, and he felt her quiver in his arms. "We're going to head to the food court and maybe check out a couple of those souvenir shops. Don't look at him and don't lose your cool. There's probably another man by the front gate."

A rush of adrenaline shot through his system, but he tamped it down. It was what he missed most about his previous jobs—the chase, the thrill of excitement and the chance that only one man would be left standing in the end. Shane grabbed Rachel by the hand and they strolled to the food court, stopping to grab an ice cream on the way.

Shane picked up another follower out of the corner of his eye and squeezed Rachel's hand when she started to turn and look at him. "You've only got eyes for me, Sugar."

"That's a hell of an ego you have."

"I'll be glad to back it up once we get out of here."

The sun was shining and Shane thought it was probably close to eighty degrees outside, but both men wore lightweight jackets to cover their shoulder holsters. Not good. The last thing he wanted to do was give them reason to open fire in such a crowded place.

Shane spotted several souvenir shops that were overrun with tour groups, and he gently pushed Rachel into the crowd. The air was cool inside the shops and sent chills over his sweat slicked skin. Tables were filled to overflowing with t-shirts and knick-knacks, so he took his cap off and put it on a display table and replaced it with a straw hat, hoping it would buy them some time. He didn't stop to look over his shoulder, though the itch at the back of his neck had turned into a burn. Shane picked up the pace when he saw an employee entrance behind one of the souvenir shops that led to a parking lot, and he kept Rachel in front of him, protecting her body with his own.

People scrambled and screams filled the air as the first sound of gunfire rang out behind him.

"Go, go!" he yelled to Rachel. "Stay low."

Wood splintered above Shane's head and a splinter sliced his cheek. Blood dripped steadily down his face, but he ignored it and kept his eye on the prize—a way out and their only chance for survival. He knocked over tables as he passed them and souvenirs littered the aisles.

Shane and Rachel pushed through the door at the back of the shop and the bright sun left tiny spots dancing in front of his eyes, but they forged ahead, adrenaline and instinct taking over. Another shot rang out and chips of concrete exploded in a cloud of dust at their feet.

"Almost there," Shane said, eyeing the gate of chain link that led into the employee parking lot at the back of the zoo. Sirens roared in the distance, overpowering the screams and sobs of the crowd behind him. Rachel ran full force into the gate and it swung open with a violent clang of metal hitting metal. The gate crashed behind him and he knew the men were hot on their heels.

"Keep running. Don't look back," he said to Rachel.

Shane hovered his body over hers and pushed her between a row of parked cars, forcing them both to their knees on the hot pavement. Rachel's breath was labored and her eyes were wide with fear, but she was hanging in there. Shane pulled a snub-nosed revolver from his ankle holster and listened as the footsteps of the men in pursuit slowed. There were still just two men, and Shane heard them split up so they could cover more ground.

The seconds ticking by seemed like hours and he knew there would only be a short window of opportunity for them to escape. He and Rachel crawled between the cars, listening as the footsteps drifted closer, then farther away as the men crept up and down each aisle.

Shane slipped a small, thin tool from his pocket and went to work on the silver Taurus they were hiding beside. The lock snicked and he opened the door softly, pushing Rachel across the seat to the passenger side and then following her inside. He pushed her down, so she was hunkered on the floorboard, and he removed the plastic panel from the underside of the steering wheel.

The footsteps were getting closer again and sweat snaked down his spine as he touched bare wires together. The car rumbled to life and he pushed down on the accelerator. Tires squealed and the smell of burned rubber was overpowering as he shot out of the parking space. A bullet pinged off the back bumper and then another shattered a taillight. Shane pulled the drivers side door shut and sat up slowly as he put more space between them and the gunmen. He glanced in the rearview mirror and saw the men slow to a stop. One of them already had a cell phone in his hand, probably relaying the license plate of the car they'd stolen.

Rachel sat up in her seat and calmly fastened her seatbelt once they were back on the highway. "I guess we're going to be a few minutes late meeting Mr. Marsh."

Shane looked over at her. Her hair was mussed, her clothes were torn and there was dirt smeared on the side of her face, but there was a sparkle in her eyes that told him she was glad to be alive. He pulled the car to the side of the road and pulled her into his arms before he could think better of it. He took her lips in a scorching kiss and fought for control over his body as he felt her melt against him, accepting him. Shane pushed her away from him before he lost it completely and pulled back into traffic.

"You're a hell of a woman, Rachel Valentine."

CHAPTER FIVE

Dusk was slowly creeping over the city by the time they'd found another vehicle. Smog was thick and glowed an eerie orange haze as the last rays of light disappeared. They'd found a green Ford Explorer in an overnight parking garage and taken it as a sign of luck. Traffic was congested as they wove their way down one-way streets and between skyscrapers, and Rachel breathed a sigh of relief as they got closer to her goal and freedom.

She'd had eight months to decide what she could do with her life once the axe hanging over her head had disappeared. New Orleans had felt like home from the moment she'd entered the city, and she knew it's where she would return. Maybe she'd even open her own design business. But those dreams were still a lifetime away.

"I had to leave the bag with my weapons and

most of the money in the pickup truck," Shane said, disturbing her private thoughts. The more she was around Shane Quincy, the more disturbing he became. He was an odd combination—all male, potently virile in a way that made women gravitate towards him, and his protective instincts only enhanced his appeal. But though those traits were attractive to Rachel, they weren't the ones that made her want to open herself to Shane Quincy like she had to no other man. He was wounded, a tortured soul, and Rachel recognized the symptoms in Shane only because she lived with them in herself.

"Did you hear me?" he asked. "We have little money and no guns."

"I have a feeling you're trying to tell me something," Rachel said finally giving him her full attention.

"I'm telling you we have to get where we're going on the money I have in my pocket, or until I can get in touch with my friend and have him meet me with a few necessities. I don't want to take the chance of being seen by going back to the zoo and trying to retrieve the bag, and I especially don't want to bodyguard my client with a piss-ant .22 and six bullets."

"No, that doesn't really inspire a lot of confidence. Can't you have your office send you the things you need?"

"Anything they send can be easily traced. I've got good security, but people will be watching my office closely since your pal shot the hell out of it. My old squadron leader from the Marines will get us everything we need without alerting anyone."

The Explorer turned right at a stoplight and passed the offices of Decker and Marsh.

"There's the parking garage," Rachel pointed out. She looked at the clock on the dash and noticed it was past six o'clock. "I hope he's still waiting. He's not the most patient man, especially where I'm concerned."

"Looks like everyone has cleared out for the evening," Shane said.

The Explorer turned into the parking garage, and Rachel saw nothing but concrete and empty parking spaces. Thick pillars sat parallel to each other like stone soldiers as they drove up the ramps to each level.

"Dammit, why does he have to be so difficult? Would it have killed him to wait half and hour? I don't know how to get in touch with him out of the office. His home and cell number are in my phone back in New Orleans."

"Well, hell. That is a problem, Sugar."

Rachel watched as Shane unhooked the .22 from his ankle rig and put it on the console between them. "What's wrong? I don't see anyone following us."

They climbed higher. The shadows grew darker and dread settled in the pit of Rachel's stomach. There were too many places for one man to hide.

"It's my fault. I've been a little busy since your apartment caught fire yesterday, and I didn't ask all the questions I should have before we started out together. I guarantee whoever shot at us in New Orleans has already searched what's left of your apartment. They'll have your cell phone and any personal contacts you had in it, and they'll be searching for them."

"Oh my God, what have I done? I don't have many people's information in my phone because I don't have that many close friends, but my roommate from college and a friend who had the apartment across from mine in Chicago are in there. I have to call them and warn them."

"As soon as we get out of here," Shane promised.

Her Uncle Angelo was ruthless, and she prayed it wasn't too late to save Cleo and Randy's lives. Angelo would leave no stone unturned until he had what he wanted.

They reached the top level of the parking garage and a lone black Mercedes was parked in the corner. The lights were dim and yellow and the Explorer's engine seemed excessively loud in the quiet.

"I don't know what kind of car he drives," Rachel said.

"Only one way to find out."

They parked the Explorer cross-wise behind the Mercedes so they still had easy access to the exit.

"Leave your door open. Just in case," he told her.

Rachel got out of the car and met Shane around the other side. The .22 was down at his side and his expression was grim. When she looked at the car she understood why. Splatters of blood patterned across the windshield, and a body was hunched over the wheel.

It was a lot of blood.

"Stay back," Shane said and moved in front of her.

Rachel appreciated the gesture, but now wasn't the time to get squeamish. Now was the time to find the papers and get the hell out of Dodge. "That's him," she said as she walked around the car to get a better look at the victim's face.

"Dammit, Rachel. I told you to stay back."

"So I have to make you mad before you use my name instead of calling me Sugar. Something I'll have to remember for the future. Let's get something straight, Buttercup. I've hired you to protect my life, not my sensibilities. We have more important things to worry about besides whether or not I lose my lunch. I've got to find those papers."

"Whatever you say," Shane said, putting his hands up. "I always try to accommodate the client, since you're the one paying the bills."
Rachel couldn't help making him angry. It was better than breaking down in front of him and crying her eyes out, which is exactly what she wanted to do. She might be Dominic Valentine's daughter, but this was the first dead body she'd ever seen. And she hoped it would be the last.

"His briefcase is open on the passenger seat." Rachel reached for the door handle.

"Don't touch anything," Shane said tersely.

Rachel jerked her hand away from the door handle, surprised by the hardness in Shane's voice. She watched as he went back to the Explorer and dug around until he found a couple of tissues in the glove compartment.

"Thanks," she said as she took one from him. "I wasn't thinking about fingerprints."

"That's why you pay me the big bucks, Sugar. We don't want to give local law enforcement a reason to look for us. If the FBI got wind of it, it would make things very difficult for the rest of our trip."

"Right. Because so far things have been a breeze," Rachel said testily. She was hurt by the harshness of his words and knew it was only a matter of time before she couldn't pretend that the sight of Galen Marsh didn't bother her. She used the tissue to open the door handle and found it unlocked.

The stench of death assaulted her as soon as she opened the door, and she held her arm in front of her mouth and nose to try and lessen it. But the cloying smell lingered in the back of her throat, no matter how hard she tried to get rid of it. She stepped back from the car and took a deep breath, focusing on what she had to do next.

Shane stood to the side, his expression challenging and devoid of all other emotion. It didn't look like he was going to offer a helping hand this time around. Well, she'd asked for it, though she hadn't thought he'd be able to cut off all his emotions like they were attached to a switch. She was Dominic Valentine's daughter. She could do anything she set her mind to.

Rachel held her breath and bent back into the car, careful not to touch the red stains that sat in liquid pools around the body. Marsh's briefcase lay open on the passenger seat and papers were scattered everywhere. All of them were splattered with blood. She made the mistake of looking at his face. His eyes were empty and stared straight at her, and his hair was matted with drying blood.

Rachel backed out of the car and collapsed to the ground, shoving her head between her knees as the little black dots began swimming in front of her eyes. She lost track of time as she tried to get herself under control, but she vaguely heard Shane sifting through papers, doing the job she should have been able to do.

"I don't see any envelopes," Shane said after a few minutes. "It looks like someone beat us to it, and now it's time for us to disappear."

Her stomach still felt queasy and she wasn't sure her legs would hold her if she tried to stand. "Shouldn't we call the police?"

"Not unless you want to go to jail. I wouldn't be surprised if this was a trap so we could be detained until your uncle's FBI insider can find us and do damage control. Get in the car."

Rachel let Shane help her to her feet and push her toward the Explorer. The sound of sirens was audible somewhere in the distance, and Shane didn't waste any time sticking around to find out.

Rachel barely had time to close her door and grab onto the door handle before Shane floored the Explorer. They sped down the narrow ramps at a neck-breaking pace and took the turns on two wheels. The squeal of tires echoed off the concrete walls, and they shot out of the garage onto the main road like a bullet out of a pistol.

The first squad car pulled into the garage, red and blue lights flashing and siren blaring, just as they turned the corner.

"You're insane," Rachel said, trying to control her breathing.

"Hey, it's all part of the bodyguard package. You're still alive aren't you?"

It was obvious Shane was still angry about the comment she'd made earlier. And if she wasn't mistaken, he wasn't just angry. He was hurt.

"Look, I'm sorry if I seemed ungrateful back there. I know you were just trying to help, but I've been on my own for a long time. I'm not used to white knights charging to the rescue, and it's obvious you have this need to save and protect when someone's in trouble. I'll be the first to admit I was wrong back there. I wasn't prepared for it, and I didn't handle it like I thought I'd be able to."

"You did okay, Sugar. And I hate to disappoint you, but I'm nobody's white knight. Never have been. Never will be."

Rachel saw his jaw clench as he navigated them through the streets and back onto the highway. If she had dared to touch him, she knew he would have been cold as marble. What was going on in the mind of Shane Quincy? Was he really as heartless and detached as he wanted her to believe? She couldn't believe that she'd read him wrong after he'd risked his life saving her from the fire.

"Can we just agree that we're both approaching new territory and call a truce?" she finally said.

"Fine with me. I'd prefer to drop it if it's all the same to you. Marsh is dead, and as far as the list is concerned, it looks like we're on our way to Chicago," Shane said. "Unless you sent a copy to someone else."

"No one else has a copy."

Shane blew out a breath and smiled, his lips thin and hard. "Well, Sugar, it looks like we're about to jump out of the frying pan and into the fire. And maybe we'll both come out alive."

"With an attitude like that, Sugar," Rachel said with brow raised, "It's a wonder you have any clients at all."

Jimmy Grabbaldi waited until the dark green Explorer turned the corner before he started the engine of the nondescript, beige Volvo he'd gotten from the rental company. Angelo Valentine was not happy with Jimmy's performance so far, and Jimmy was already dreading his punishment. Nobody screwed up Angelo Valentine's plans and got away with it. Not even one of his top men.

He'd lost Rachel and the private detective once

they'd left New Orleans, and all he had to show for his efforts were sixteen stitches in the side of his cheek where he'd been cut by a piece of flying brick after Rachel had shot at him. She was going to have to pay for that. His only option had been to head back to her apartment and wait until the scene was clear so he could do a little investigating of his own. And he'd hit pay dirt.

He'd immediately called Angelo and told him what had happened. The silence on the other end of the line had sent chills down his spine. Angelo Valentine could say a lot without uttering a word. Angelo had ordered him back to Chicago and was going to send a more competent person in his place, and that's when Jimmy had told him what he'd found in Rachel's apartment.

He'd gotten her phone off the nightstand and found the list of people she trusted enough to stay in contact with, even though she was in hiding. There had only been three contacts in her in her address book, two friends and her attorney, and Jimmy had relayed the information to Angelo with satisfaction. There was no doubt in Jimmy's mind that any acquaintances of Rachel's would be "taken care" of.

In exchange for the information Jimmy provided, Angelo decided to let him continue his search for Rachel. The FBI informant who was working on the inside for the Valentine organization had relayed the information that Rachel and her new boyfriend had been in contact with an attorney who had access to the list. Jimmy's new assignment had been obvious, and he'd immediately headed to Dallas.

The freelance goons Angelo had hired had failed to kill Rachel and her boyfriend at the zoo, but Jimmy didn't worry too much about Rachel. Her time would come—just as Galen Marsh's had. Galen Marsh hadn't died with dignity. But more importantly, Marsh hadn't had a chance to give the list to Rachel.

Jimmy kept his eye on the Explorer in front of him as they merged into traffic on the highway headed north. He hit the speed dial on his phone and turned it on speaker.

"Mr. Grabbaldi. I hope you're calling me with good news." Angelo Valentine had the voice of a demon. It was the only thing Jimmy could think of as sweat pooled at the base of his neck and ran in rivulets down his temples. Angelo's voice was low and gravely due to a throat injury he'd suffered as a young man, but there was nothing weak about it.

"Yes, sir. I've picked up Rachel Valentine and her friend in Dallas just as the informant told you. They're headed north. I'll wait until they stop for the night to take them out."

"Good, good. And what about the other little problem? I assume you had no problems with that job."

"Mr. Marsh is taken care of, sir, and the papers have been recovered."

"Excellent, Mr. Grabbaldi. Destroy them immediately. I may decide to let you live after all." There was a pause over the line and Jimmy could hear Angelo breathing. "Then again, maybe not."

"Yes, sir," Jimmy said as the spit dried up in his mouth, making it difficult to swallow.

"Don't let them get to Chicago, Mr. Grabbaldi. Rachel Valentine has another copy of the list somewhere. Don't fail me."

The line went dead and Jimmy deliberately relaxed his cramping fingers from around the steering wheel. Rachel Valentine was headed into Oklahoma. It was the quickest way to get across the border and lose the interest of any local law enforcement. He knew from experience that Rachel and her private detective would be stuck on a two lane road for hours. He'd have to be careful not to be seen.

Jimmy turned the radio on the classical station to soothe his nerves and plan his future. He had a nice fat bank account in the Caymans, and he figured it was time for Jimmy Grabbaldi to retire. Killing Rachel Valentine would be his last job. He wasn't going to tempt fate and give Angelo the chance to change his mind about letting him live.

CHAPTER SIX

Shane waited in the car and kept an eye on Rachel as she used a payphone to call her friends. By the agitated way she kept wrapping the phone cord around her wrist, it didn't look like she was having a lot of luck reaching them. If Angelo Valentine had put a hit out on Rachel's friends, Shane felt sure they didn't have much of a chance for survival. But he wasn't going to be the one to say so.

They were stopped at a gas station on the Texas/Oklahoma border. It was the last place to get gas for more than two hours, but Shane had another reason for stopping. He wanted to see if the beige sedan he'd spotted in his rearview mirror was really following them. Shane tried to get a good look at the driver, but the sedan motored past them without giving them a glance.

Rachel got back into the Explorer and Shane

thought she looked close to tears. She'd had a rough twenty-four hours, and it wasn't over yet. Neither of them had slept and their clothes were torn and dirty.

"You can try to call them again once we find a place to stay for the night," Shane said.

"I know. It's just that they're clueless as to what I've gotten them involved in, and they have no way of protecting themselves. It was stupid of me not to cut all ties completely, but I couldn't face leaving everything and everyone I've ever known behind all at once."

Her words struck a chord with Shane. Isn't that exactly what he'd done after his wife had died and he'd left the FBI? He hadn't spoken to any of his friends since the funeral. Wildcat, Dixon, Cutter, Jax, Doc and Merlin—men who had guarded his back and been there for him in the toughest of times. He'd turned his back on them all. He'd packed up his meager belongings and left Washington without looking back. He'd picked New Orleans simply by closing his eyes and pointing to a place on the map. Guilt and shame crept its way over him and he promised himself then and there that he'd make amends as soon as Rachel Valentine was safe.

It was full dark as they crossed the border and headed north through Oklahoma. The silence was heavy, each of them lost in their own thoughts. Shane figured it would be close to midnight by the time they reached Tulsa. It was the closest city he knew of that would have a place to eat and an available motel. It was risky stopping for the night, but Rachel couldn't go on much longer. And even though he could go on as long as the mission required, sleep and food would fuel his body and keep him alert.

"Did you get in touch with your FBI friend?" Rachel asked, breaking the silence.

That was another reason Shane had wanted to stop before they entered a new state. He knew his calls to Jones Daugherty at FBI Headquarters in Chicago would be traced. And he'd been right. He'd heard the clicks on the other end of the line that told him the call was being traced, and as soon as Wildcat had come on the line the conversation had been short and sweet.

"Yeah, I used the payphone while you were in the bathroom. Jones gave me a private number to call as soon as we get to a place I can talk for awhile. He could tell I was in a hurry and needed to get off the line before they could pinpoint a location."

"Don't take this the wrong way, but are you sure you can trust this guy? How do you know he isn't the informant working on the inside for Uncle Angelo?"

"Some things you just know. Wildcat has saved my life on more than one occasion and I've saved his. I'd trust him with my life and yours, too. He's good people."

"I guess that's good enough for me," she said.

"Why don't you try to get some sleep," Shane said. "We've got a long drive ahead of us."

"Are you kidding me? As soon as we crossed the border into Oklahoma I've felt like we were in that movie."

"Lost Highway?"

"No, Deliverance. I haven't seen a town, a streetlight, a restaurant or another car for hours. It's like we've entered into the Twilight Zone. And I don't mean to be a pest, but I haven't eaten anything since lunch and I'm starving. I know you're a macho tough guy and could probably sustain yourself by picking grass from the side of the road, but us weaklings have to have real sustenance."

"Like a cheeseburger?" Shane asked, laughing as her stomach picked that moment to rumble loudly.

"Yeah, a cheeseburger would be good."

"We'll be in Tulsa before too long. We can stop there and grab a bite to eat before bunking down for the night."

Shane settled back into comfortable silence and looked out into the night. He'd been all over the world, and it always amazed him to see how different the sky looked. He'd been in third world countries and drug-run jungles, but he'd never seen a sky as black as the one over him right now. No stars shone in the sky and the moon was just a sliver of pale dust. The land wasn't cluttered with modern technology—no oil wells, power lines, self-service gas stations or cell phone service. It was just open, empty land.

Almost an hour had passed in silence when Rachel sat up in her seat and squealed. It wasn't a sound he'd heard before, and he was already checking the rearview mirror and increasing their speed, his gun clutched comfortably in his right hand while he searched for danger.

"Oh, my God," she said, pulling on his shirt sleeve like a child. "Do you see it?"

"See what?" he asked, wondering if she was hallucinating because of lack of sleep.

"The lights. All the glorious lights," she said. "Stay with me, Quincy. The lights mean there's civilization—food, a shower, a soft bed. Don't tell me you're not excited about the prospects that lie ahead of us. Tulsa is my new favorite city."

Shane didn't want to think about Rachel Valentine and a soft bed in the same sentence together. Which posed another problem. How the hell he was going to share a room with her? Even after everything she'd been through in the last twenty-four hours, she was still the most beautiful woman he'd ever seen. He had it bad.

"Step on it man. Your client is hungry and in

need of a shower. And you did say you always try to please the client."

"Yes, maam," Shane said. He was lighter of heart than he'd been in a long time, and it was all because he was on the run from a madman with a woman he was afraid he could fall in love with. It was fortunate he had no plans to go down that path, or he'd be in real trouble.

Rachel's stomach rumbled again as Shane pulled into the lot of a twenty-four hour diner attached to what could at best be called a "seedy" motel—minus the "M." Jake's otel was as basic as you could get. It was a rectangle of sandy-colored, crumbling brick trimmed with turquoise paint. There were two floors and twenty-four rooms with stairs at each end, and each room had one window. A soft drink machine sat in the middle of the sidewalk with an "out of order" sign taped to it.

"You sure know how to show a girl a good time, Quincy."

"That's what they tell me. But this will have to do until Jones can supply me with some more cash."

"My eyes are going to be closed anyway, so it's not like I'll actually see the roaches crawling around on the floor."

"That's the spirit," he said.

They got out of the Explorer and headed toward the diner. “It’s getting colder,” Rachel said, rubbing her bare arms.

The wind had picked up and the air smelled of ozone. Static lay heavy in the air. “Looks like we’ll get a thunderstorm before the night’s over. I hope *Jake’s otel* can handle a little rain.”

The diner was empty when they went inside. Fluorescent lights flickered overhead and cracked vinyl booths with scarred Formica tabletops lined the walls. The floor was black and white checked squares, dingy with what looked liked years of scuff marks and soda spills.

A lone waitress with bottle thick glasses and permed brown hair that frizzed away from her face sat perched on a stool behind the register. Her age was somewhere between thirty-five and sixty-five. The lights weren’t flattering. She was doing a crossword puzzle and gave them no more than a cursory glance when they entered. Her sigh of annoyance could be heard all over the restaurant.

“How you folks doin’ tonight,” she said as she grabbed a couple of greasy menus and led them to a corner booth.

“Fine, thank you,” Rachel said politely.

“The name’s Nadine. Coffee’s fresh and bottomless if you want it. Or we got other stuff.”

“Coffee’s fine with me,” Shane answered.

“Just water for me,” Rachel said. “And I already know I want the biggest cheeseburger you have with a side of fries.”

“Make that two,” Shane said, before the waitress had a chance to lay the greasy menu in front of him.

“Comin’ right out, folks,” Nadine said and shuffled away.

“I’m going to wash up in the bathroom and see if I can find a phone to use,” Rachel said. “I won’t rest easy until I get in touch Cleo and Randy and know they’re safe.”

Shane waited until she disappeared and moved to a position where he could see both the bathroom and the front doors. The parking lot was still empty other than the green Explorer, but he didn’t want t take any chances. He pulled out a slip of paper from his wallet that held the number Jones had given him earlier that evening and he used one of the disposable cell phones.

“What the hell have you gotten involved in, Ace?” Jones Daugherty asked as he came on the line. Ace had been Shane’s nickname in the Marines because of his ability to hit his target with complete accuracy.

“You’re name’s come up with a red flag all over the FBI. Word has it your apartment building was torched, your business was destroyed and you're wanted for questioning as a person of interest in the murder of a high profile attorney in Dallas. And all because of a woman. Sounds like you should have stayed in the FBI. Going independent has obviously made you forget how to follow the rules."

"Yeah, well, you shouldn't listen to gossip. And I was never that good at following rules, anyway."

"I know that better than anyone," Jones said with a laugh.

"As far as what you've heard, my apartment wasn't damaged in the fire, it was my neighbor's. Insurance will cover the damage to my business and somebody else had already killed the lawyer before we got there. But I can confirm a hundred percent that it all happened because of a woman."

"Tell me," Wildcat ordered.

"Rachel Valentine is in my protection, and let's just say that her uncle doesn't think that's such a good idea. And after our trip to Dallas, I'm beginning to think someone in the FBI doesn't think it's such a good idea either."

Nothing but silence greeted Shane from the other end. "You still there, Wildcat?"

"I've done an internal investigation on every agent in the Bureau who was ever involved with the Valentines. You know how big that list is. You were on the original task force."

Shane winced. "Don't remind me."

"I've found no evidence that there's someone working for Angelo Valentine on the inside. And believe me, I've looked. I've looked hard."

"Just keep your eyes open."

"Roger, that. Where are you now?"

"We're in Tulsa for the night, but we'll head out early in the morning. I've got to figure out some way to get Rachel to the bank in Chicago and get the papers out of her lock box before anyone knows we're there."

"Fat chance of that happening. I've heard it through the grapevine that people are expecting you to show up here eventually. You'll have to be a ghost to get past Angelo's men, not to mention the FBI alert that's out on you."

"I don't suppose you'd be inclined to help an old friend?" Shane asked.

"What, and risk losing this glamorous job? I could probably be persuaded to help you out. But it'll cost you. And you might not like the favor when it comes down to it."

"You always were a perverse bastard," Shane said. "But you leave me with no choice but to agree. And look on the bright side. If you get fired I'll even find a place for you on my staff. My secretary is getting close to retirement. How are your typing skills?"

Shane smiled as Jones laughed and uttered a crude suggestion. "In all seriousness, Wildcat, I really appreciate your help. You don't owe me anything. I haven't exactly been the greatest friend over the last couple of years, but I'm grateful all the same."

"What the hell kind of Dr. Phil psychobabble is that? I expect a man is inclined to go off on his own every now and then. There are some things in the world that change and some things that don't. Try to remember that. Now tell me what you need me to do."

Shane felt the grip of guilt release around his heart. He'd been afraid his lack of interest in his friends, hell, his lack of interest in life after his wife's death had screwed things up with Wildcat past the point of no return. But Wildcat was acting like the years hadn't passed at all, and Shane was grateful.

"Well, for starters, I need guns and plenty of ammunition. I'll also need a couple of Flak jackets and infrared goggles. You know what I prefer. And I need enough cash to buy basic supplies and get us where we need to go."

"Anything else?" Jones asked.

"I need to take a look at the files you've collected on each agent working the Valentine case. The insider is there somewhere, and Rachel will never be safe as long as that person is running around. I also need a safe house if you've got one available close enough to Chicago so the trip can be made in less than an hour. It'll give us a place to stay until I figure out what the hell we're going to do."

"If anyone finds out about this you know my ass is grass," Jones said, "but I'll see what I can do. Give me till noon tomorrow. You should be able to make it to St. Louis, Missouri by then if you leave at dawn. I'll meet you in the parking lot of the Galleria just outside of Nordstrom. They're doing a lot of construction and the lot will be crowded. I'll be in a black Tahoe."

The line went dead and Shane slipped the phone into his pocket. Rachel took her seat across from him and he could tell by the look on her face that she still hadn't been able to get in touch with her friends.

"No luck?" he asked. Nadine took that moment to deliver their cheeseburgers and refill his coffee.

"No, just an answering machine at both places. I didn't leave a message."

Shane took a bite of his food. Grease dripped onto his plate, and he watched Rachel try to avoid the same problem by cutting hers in half. Grease dripped down her chin and onto her arm at the first bite.

"I don't want to hear a word," she said, laughing.

"I'm hungry enough to not care about what's in this burger."

When they were finished Shane pulled out his wallet and left enough to cover the check and a tip. "Let's see what our neighborhood motel has to offer."

They walked outside to the Explorer and drove around the diner and the motel to the front office. The city was silent and the streets empty. Cars were scattered sporadically in the parking lot, enough to tell Shane that Jake's otel probably did a lot of business by the hour. A lone streetlight glowed yellow in the parking lot, and a flashing neon sign declared vacancies.

Lightning streaked across the sky and the first rumbles of thunder grumbled in the distance.

Shane opened the cracked glass door of the office and ushered Rachel in front of him. The smell of stale cigarettes and burnt coffee was overwhelming. A small black and white T.V. sat in the corner with foil wrapped around the antennae and the volume turned all the way down. A man sat in a threadbare recliner and didn't take his eyes away from the screen as the bell rang above the door.

"Excuse me," Shane said as the man continued to sit in his chair and stare at the T.V. "We'd like a room for the night."

"It's thirty-seven fifty for the night. Twenty for an hour. Sign your name in the book, and take a key off the hook. Checkout's at eleven."

Sometimes things worked out the way they were supposed to, Shane thought. He wouldn't even have to bribe the man to keep their names out of the register. Shane left two twenty's on the counter and didn't bother signing the book. He took the key off the hook for the room at the very end on the bottom floor. Room number twenty-three. It was hidden behind two large dumpsters and would give them a little coverage if they had to make a sudden exit.

Shane didn't bother to thank the guy as they left the musty office. He left the Explorer parked where it was so as not to give their room location away and grabbed a small sack of toiletries and two clean shirts (one in each of their sizes) he'd bought when he'd stopped at the Wal-Mart in Texas to buy clothes for Rachel.

"I don't suppose you've got clean sheets in that little sack, do you?" Rachel asked.

"Nope. Toothbrushes, toothpaste, soap, shampoo, a hair brush, deodorant and clean shirts. No sheets."

"Darn. I hate to tell you this, but I don't think I'm brave enough to stay in *Jake's otel*. Maybe we could find a nice cardboard box in an alley somewhere."

"Think of it as an adventure. If you can survive the night here, then you can survive the mob." Shane stuck the key in the lock and pushed open the door.

The air inside the room was stuffy and stale. He flicked on the light switch and immediately wished he could take back the action.

"I've always thought hot pink and turquoise compliment each other," Rachel said.

Shane shut the door behind him and immediately locked the deadbolt and put on the chain. He pulled the curtains closed so no outside glare from the street lights was let in. "What about the brown and orange bedspread. What does that compliment?" he asked.

"I'm not sure that bedspread would compliment the flames I'd like to burn it with."

The room was barely large enough to hold the furniture inside. A large king-size bed dominated the room and a small table and chairs sat in the corner. A small door led into a closet-sized bathroom and there were hooks on the wall to hang clothes instead of a closet.

Shane went about turning the fan on and putting the toiletries in the bathroom, noticing that Rachel still stood in front of the door chewing on her bottom lip. She was staring at the king-sized bed like it was leading her down the path to hell, and he had to bite the inside of his cheek to keep from laughing when she spotted the circular mirror on the ceiling.

He knew exactly what she was feeling because the bed had given him more than a moment of concern, but as long as he remembered that she was a client and he was being paid to protect her, all thoughts of wanting to make love to her disappeared. Or at least mostly disappeared. He'd have to be dead not to think of it a little.

"Why don't you go ahead and take the first shower? You look dead on your feet," he said while he unhooked his ankle holster and put the .22 on the nightstand closest to the door.

"Yeah, okay," she said, still staring at the bed. "So I guess you're planning for both of us to sleep there."

"Unless you want to sleep in the tub. Don't worry, your virtue will stay intact. I never take advantage of a client."

"So I guess the kiss you gave me earlier was saying something like, 'Way to go, pal,'" she said with a raised eyebrow and quirk of lips.

"Just take your shower. We've got to be up at dawn and on our way to St. Louis."

"I take it your friend has agreed to help us?"

"Yes. He'll have everything we need and give us a place to stay for a couple of days while we're trying to figure out the mess of how to get you to Chicago in one piece. Don't use all the hot water," Shane said and lay back on the bed fully clothed.

Rachel went into the bathroom and grimaced at the avocado green fixtures. At least the color probably hid the mold well. A dingy shower curtain hung limply from a tarnished rod and she jerked it open quickly, expecting to see either a knife-wielding maniac or a spider the size of her fist. She blew out a breath of relief when she saw neither.

Rachel took her clothes off in the tub so she wouldn't have to stand in her bare feet on the grimy tile and folded her ruined clothes over the back of the toilet. She turned the water on and was thankful that at least the hot water worked and came out of the shower nozzle in more than a trickle. If she closed her eyes, she was pretty sure standing in the moldy shower of Jake's Hotel was the best experience she'd had in a long time.

Fatigue was starting to take its toll, so she washed her hair and body quickly and then turned the water off. A rod on the wall held two paper thin towels, so she grabbed one and dried her body quickly and then wrapped the towel around her sopping head. She washed her underwear in the sink and hung it to dry over the rod and slipped on the plain white t-shirt Shane had bought her. It barely covered her backside, but it was the only thing she had to sleep in. Sleeping next to Shane was enough temptation in itself. What she really needed was full body armor and a chastity belt.

Rachel left the light on in the bathroom and made her way to her side of the bed quickly, slipping under the covers before Shane had a chance to glance in her direction. She didn't know that Shane had noticed everything about her—how the shirt clung to her damp body or how long her legs were.

She fell asleep blissfully unaware that she was torturing her protector.

CHAPTER SEVEN

The late afternoon sun baked the city and tortured pedestrians as they scurried to their destinations. Washington was in the middle of a heat wave, the hottest the city had seen in years, and beads of sweat ran down Shane's temples and into his eyes—the salt stinging and the sun glaring.

The Federal Reserve Building on Constitution Avenue was full of people just after lunch—tour groups, employees and government officials. He was positioned on top of the Roosevelt building across the street. Black tar from the roof stuck to his clothes and his rifle was set on a tripod stand aimed at the building. He had a perfect view to the inside of the building through his scope.

The gunman had gathered all of the hostages and made them sit in the center of the room, legs crossed and hands flat on the floor. It had only taken a glance through the scope to see the people were terrified—children from a tour group sat huddled in fear and the men and women around them tried to offer comfort and dry their tears.

His wife stood out like a beacon. An authority figure who was in complete control, though he could tell by the way she rubbed her hands on her black skirt that she was nervous. But she didn't show her captor fear. Her posture was straight and defiant and her expression angry as she followed the gunman's every movement.

A negotiator was called in to speak with the gunman, but the standard tactics weren't working. The gunman was becoming more agitated with every call. He paced back and forth across the marble tile like a caged animal, the people at his feet forgotten and his demands growing stronger. Minutes turned into hours and the heat intensified as the sun crept higher.

A car alarm blared from down the block and a chopper circled overhead. The smell of hot tar and exhaust made the inside of his nose raw as he looked through the scope of his rifle. The streets were cordoned off around the building. The gunman had asked for an armored truck to load gold bars into, and it sat big and black and shiny in front of the Federal Reserve Building. The gunman picked hostages to load the truck and then had them return to the bank and sit back down on the floor.

The gunman grabbed a woman from the floor and used her as a shield as he began to leave the building. From all appearances, it looked like he was going to let the other hostages go.

"Fire when ready," Director Hudson ordered Shane. "I don't want the bastard to step foot outside of that building. We don't need any more of a media circus than we've already got."

"What about the hostage?" Shane asked, his voice hollow.

"Take the shot, Quincy," Director Hudson ordered again, and Shane knew the life of the woman wasn't as important as the bigger picture to a man like Hudson.

But Shane followed orders. His finger was steady on the trigger as he slowly pulled it back. The rifle jerked in his arms and the bullet cut through the waves of heat pouring up from the pavement as if it were in slow motion. The gunman was unsuspecting, his focus on the struggling woman and getting them both to the truck.

The other hostages were restless and beginning to stand, relieved the ordeal was over. The crack of the rifle firing was delayed, the bullet faster than the speed of sound, and Shane watched as it sliced through the glass doors of the Federal Reserve and into the gunman's heart, missing the woman by only a fraction of an inch. But in the end it hadn't mattered. She'd died anyway.

Real time whooshed back in an instant as the man fell to his knees. The city was still, a void in space, and then all hell broke loose. The explosion rocketed through the front of the building, engulfing it in black smoke and flame. Debris rained from the sky and large chunks of concrete catapulted into the street, damaging cars and breaking the windows of the surrounding buildings. The lives of so many people had meant less than 400 ounce rectangles of metal.

Shane's life as he'd known it had ended in an instant.

He woke gasping for air and his skin slicked with sweat. He was disoriented and cold and his muscles cramped in fear. And when a soft hand touched him on the shoulder he had to fight to keep from jumping out of the bed like a coward.

"Shane?" Rachel asked.

He didn't answer her. Couldn't answer her. The soft hand began rubbing slow circles over his back until his breathing slowed. Rain pounded against the window and thunder cracked loudly, shaking the glass.

"Shane? Are you okay?" she asked again.

"Yeah, just give me a minute." The dream was always the same. He'd killed his wife. Killed all of those people. The children. Despite the higher ups who had given him the order to fire, it had been only his finger on the trigger. Not theirs.

"Do you want to talk about it?"

Shane laughed sardonically and rubbed his hands across his face. "Hell, no. I lived it. Why would I want to talk about it? You sound like one of the FBI shrinks."

He was churned up, feeling mean and nasty, and he desperately wanted a bottle of Jim Beam. But he'd given up the hard stuff and taken up running instead. And now he was stuck in a motel room with a woman who made him crazy and neither of his vices were available.

Shane lay back down and turned onto his side, facing away from Rachel. The sweat on his skin was drying, leaving him clammy and cold. Rachel's fingers were driving him to distraction. He'd never considered sex as a way to chase away the bad dreams, but he was beginning to think it might not be a bad idea to take up a third vice just in case he was ever in a situation like this one again.

He hadn't touched a woman in two years, and the need rose up in him swiftly, hardening him to the point of pain. His senses were heightened—the smell of her skin and the way her breath feathered across his cheek. She snuggled up close behind him, her hand continuously soothing, while his body coiled with tension. Would she continue to soothe him if he decided to use her body and pound away his frustrations? He couldn't do that to her. Couldn't do it to anyone. No one deserved to be treated that way. Which led him back to running or Jim Beam. He choked on a laugh, but it was a sob that caught in his throat.

"I always hear you leave your apartment in the middle of the night," she said, breaking the silence. "Where do you go?"

"Running through the city. It's beautiful at night," he said, trying to think of anything but the touch of her hand or her softness pressed against him. "I tried drowning myself in alcohol for a few months, but I didn't like that version of me when I looked in the mirror any more than the version I see now. So I poured the bottles down the drain and stopped looking at myself in the mirror altogether. I didn't realize my sleep habits kept you awake."

"I'd try to stay awake until you came back, just so I could listen to you play the piano for awhile. Such sad music comes out of you, Shane. Sometimes it would make me cry."

"Well, the blues isn't meant to be happy."

"No, I suppose not, but I enjoyed hearing you all the same. You have strong hands," she said, running her fingers down the length of his arm to the tips of his fingers.

His hands were rough and his fingers calloused, but she was right. They were strong. If only the rest of his body and mind could live up to the potential. The tension slowly drained from his body with every gentle stroke of her hand. It was a comfortable feeling to wake up beside a woman in the middle of the night. He'd forgotten the intimacy, the feeling of knowing a lover's touch or the sighs that said they were dreaming peacefully. The vise around his chest loosened and he was able to breath easier. And before he could help himself, the words started pouring out of his mouth.

"I killed my wife," Shane said, expecting Rachel to distance herself from him. To slap him or gasp in horror. She did neither. She just listened.

Rachel felt sick inside. What kind of horrors had Shane been living with? She didn't believe for a moment that he'd killed his wife. He was too honorable, too loyal. He was a protector of the innocent, and his basic characteristics would never let him be anything else.

So when he dropped the bombshell about his wife, she listened with an open mind while her heart broke over the tragedy. He told her of his nightmares, and how he relived those last moments night after night, shouldering the blame for something he'd had no control over. And she listened with envy as he spoke of the woman he'd loved—her beauty, her strength and her faith in him that he was making a difference in the world.

"I've spent my entire adult life obeying someone else's orders—in the Marines and then again in the FBI," Shane said. "I've always been a pawn in someone else's game. What does that say about me that I never stopped to think for myself? That I just followed the orders of others so blindly without first thinking of all the consequences?"

"I'd say it made you the best person to do your job. The job does not define the man, Shane. You're still your own person, with your own beliefs and priorities. And no one can fault you for doing what you had to do in those last seconds."

"Well, they did fault me. And I can't blame them."

"Trying to relive history, to rethink the outcome of situations will never give you peace. You can't say for certain that he wouldn't have detonated the bomb strapped to his chest anyway. He was a sociopath. It was he who was responsible for the loss of all those lives. Not you. There are a hundred different scenarios that could have played out that day, and they all could have ended badly. From the way you described your wife I'd think she wouldn't be too happy with the way you're blaming yourself. What would she say?"

She'd probably tell him to stop moping and get the job done. "I don't know, but every day I pray that she would have forgiven me if she was still alive. She was strong. Stronger than me. Everything was black and white with Maggie. Right or wrong. There were no gray areas to get lost in. It seemed I was always skirting the gray areas in my line of work, and she'd just give me that look that said, 'Suck it up and do what's right.'"

"She sounds like an amazing woman," Rachel said.

"She was. A day doesn't go by that I don't think of her. She's my conscience. And loving her taught me something very important. That emotions always cloud the issues. I'll never let myself love anyone as whole-heartedly as I did her. The body's not meant to withstand that much torture, that much loss. It's okay to put yourself into work and relationships, but there's no reason for them to matter too much. It can only lead to disaster."

The first tear snaked down Rachel's cheek before she could stop it. Her hand had stilled on his and her breath was caught in her throat. What had she been thinking, dragging Shane into a mess of her own making and then becoming attached to him? He was everything a real man should be—honorable and trustworthy and honest. And he continued to be that way despite the pain that weighed him down. She was past the point of where she could lie to herself. She was already in love with him. How could she not be?

"Maggie would have forgiven you," she said softly, but he didn't hear her. His breathing had steadied under her hand and she realized he'd fallen asleep, the nightmares purged from his soul with his confessions. But Rachel was wide awake. And more alone than she'd ever been. She rolled away from Shane and curled into a ball, letting the tears fall silently. It was the first time she'd cried since she was a child. And all because she was in love with a man who would never love her in return.

She'd stay with Shane Quincy until the papers were safely in the possession of the FBI, and then tell him goodbye with a confidence and bravado that had come from years of practice and guidance from her father. And then she'd never look back.

CHAPTER EIGHT

Rachel woke the moment Shane left the bed. She'd spent the night tossing and turning, a deep sleep eluding her for uncomfortable dreams and thoughts of the man beside her.

The bed dipped and raised and she opened her eyes. The room was still pitched in darkness and no glimmer of morning light peaked underneath the curtains. Shane flicked on the bedside lamp and she watched the muscles in his back flex as he reached toward the ceiling in a stretch that left her mouth watering. A pair of snug boxer-briefs hugged his hips, his hair was mussed and a day's worth of beard shadowed his face. He wasn't making it easy for her to stick to her plan.

He pulled on his clothes and strapped the .22 back to his ankle, checking the cylinder even though the amount of bullets in the chamber hadn't changed since the day before. He moved around the room silently, packing up their meager belongings. He reminded her of a big cat, the way he moved so efficiently, almost lazily, but the power was coiled just beneath the surface. Always ready.

"Rise and shine, Sugar. I want to be out of here before light hits. We're supposed to meet Wildcat in St. Louis at noon."

"I'm awake. And don't call me Sugar," Rachel said as she shuffled into the bathroom to get dressed. She threw on her clothes, washed her face, brushed her teeth and pulled her hair back into a ponytail. The bags under her eyes spoke of a sleepless night and her skin was pale against the harsh lighting in the bathroom. She probably wouldn't have to worry about any more kisses from Shane.

Shane was standing by the door impatiently by the time she emerged from the bathroom, and he avoided making eye contact with her. Tension hung thick in the air between them, and words spoken in the dark of night lay heavy on both their minds.

Rachel noticed the .22 in Shane's hand.

"Stay behind me and to my right. The dumpsters will give us good coverage until we can make it to the Explorer. You ready?"

"As I'll ever be."

Shane opened the door and she followed close behind him. It took a minute for her eyes to adjust to the darkness, but it didn't look like *Jake's otel* had changed much over the last few hours. The thunderstorm had turned into a light mist and water filled the holes in the parking lot. If it was possible, *Jake's otel* looked even more pitiful than it had the night before, soggy and neglected.

They were behind the dumpsters and Rachel's pulse picked up as she thought of how long they'd be an open target on the way to the car. Her Uncle Angelo could have men placed anywhere—on the rooftops, under cars or at the liquor store across the street. She didn't like the thought of Shane putting himself in front of her. Weren't two sets of searching eyes better than one? She tried to move around him so she could see, but he stubbornly kept his body in front of hers as they edged out from behind the dumpsters.

The fine hairs on her arms and the nape of her neck prickled a moment before the gunshot rang out. Shane pushed her to the ground and into the wet, covering her body with his own. She felt his body jerk against her and they went down hard, bodies tangling. Her elbows cracked against the concrete and the breath whooshed out of her lungs, making it impossible for her to draw in a breath. Shane dropped the gun seconds before his head bounced off the pavement and his body went limp on top of hers.

Two more shots pinged off the dumpster and another hit the brick just over her head, sending shards flying.

"Shane! Shane, wake up," she said. He was dead weight on top of her and she pushed with all her might to roll him over.

He groaned as she rolled him to his side, and she could already see the lump forming on his temple. Rachel pushed to her hands and knees and felt around the knot. It was then she noticed the blood as it ran in rivulets down his arm and joined the puddles of water on the sidewalk.

"Oh, my God. Shane," she said tapping him lightly on the side of the cheek.

"Stop beating on me, woman. I'm fine. Just a knock on the head." His eyes were open now but he still looked a little unsteady.

"Oh, yeah? What about the bullet in your arm?"

He looked down at his left shoulder in surprise. "Damn. We don't have time for this. At least it looks like the bullet went all the way through."

It looked like he was losing a lot of blood to Rachel, and his hand shook as he tried to apply pressure to the wound.

"It's no big deal," he said between gritted teeth.

"The shooter must have had a night scope to have such a clear shot, but the sun's starting to come up. The direction of the sun's in our favor. There will be a glare for a few minutes as he adjusts. He'll change positions and try to trap us behind here. It's what I would do in the same situation. I need to get a pinpoint on his location and take him out. Otherwise, we're going to be sitting ducks. If something happens to me I want you to run for the car and get out of here. I'll try to stall him as long as I can."

The .22 lay on the ground. Shane's voice was getting weaker and his pupils were large and black.

"Like hell," Rachel said. "We're in this together, Quincy." She grabbed the gun from the ground and crouched low.

"Where are you, you son of a bitch?" she yelled. Shane grabbed for her, but she dodged his hand easily.

Her heart was racing and her mind was on Shane, but she knew she had to pull it together so they could both escape alive. Rachel slowed her breathing and cleared her mind like she'd been taught. It wouldn't help to think that the target was a live human being instead of a piece of paper tacked up a hundred paces away. She'd never taken a life before, but she knew she was strong enough to do what had to be done. But could she live with herself after? The little voice in the back of her mind kept asking the question, and she didn't know the answer.

The scuffle of feet moving across the pavement proved Shane's theory right. The shooter was changing positions, trying to trap them between the dumpsters and the motel. She'd have to anticipate his moves and catch him off guard. If the shooter made it to his destination they'd never make it out alive.

She concentrated on breathing and listening for the tell-tale signs of movement—the whisper of clothing as it brushed against a car, the scrape of shoes, a spent magazine falling to the ground and a new one being loaded. She glanced at Shane and saw his eyes were steady on hers. He gave her a nod of approval.

Rachel looked between the two dumpsters and caught a glimpse of a man. He was soft around the jowls and hard around the middle. Built like a boxer, with a nose to match. She didn't recognize him, but she recognized the type. He was dressed in a drab suit with a hat pulled low over his brow. He carried his weapon like he'd had lots of practice using it and had enjoyed every minute. There was no doubt in her mind he worked for Angelo Valentine.

She took aim and waited until he moved closer, but he sensed her movement and raised his gun in her direction. She had only a split second to think before she fired. His gun discharged only a moment after hers, but his aim wasn't true. The .22 stayed steady in her hand as she watched the man fall to the ground. It had been a direct hit, and she knew he wouldn't be getting up again.

Jimmy Grabbaldi should have taken retirement sooner.

When the shooting stopped, the man from the office stuck his head out the door.

"I've called the police," he yelled. "You folks had better pay for destruction of private property." He slammed the door, slid the locks into place and pulled the shades. Apparently Jake had some standards after all.

The sirens grew closer and Rachel looked down at Shane. He was losing consciousness, though the bleeding from his shoulder had turned sluggish.

"I'll be right back," she told Shane and ran out into the parking lot. She found exactly what she was looking for in the last row of the lot. A beige Volvo still had the keys dangling from the ignition. The shooter's car. She got in, turned the key and it purred to life. She drove to where Shane was lying and loaded him into the backseat.

"We've got to get you to a hospital. You've lost too much blood," she said.

"No, no hospital."

"Don't be ridiculous, Shane. You can't go on like this and last I checked I'm not a nurse. You need stitches and a brain scan, neither of which I can provide."

"No hospital," he said again. "I've had worse than this."

His wallet landed in her lap, but she didn't take her eyes off the road. She wasn't going to argue with a man who obviously had no common sense.

"There's a number in my wallet. Find a payphone and call Wildcat. Tell him what's happened and that we need an immediate safe house. I can rest there for a couple of days until I'm back on my feet."

"Shane," Rachel said, shaking her head.

"I'm trusting you to do as I ask, Rachel. The minute we step foot inside a hospital you'll have Angelo's men all over you. I'd rather die than let that happen. Promise me you'll do as I ask."

She looked at Shane in the rearview mirror. His face was pinched with pain and he was fighting to stay conscious until she agreed to his plan. She'd never forgive herself if anything happened to him, but she found herself nodding in agreement.

"I promise," she said and watched as his eyes closed and his body went slack.

Rachel waited until she was over the Missouri state line before she stopped to find a pay phone.

They'd been on the run for more than an hour without incident, but she was cautious as she pulled into a gas station in a town called Joplin. Shane was still passed out in the back seat, but his breathing was nice and steady.

She circled the block just to make sure no one was following and then turned into an Exxon station. The payphones were on the side of the building, next to the restrooms. She parked the car and took the scrap of paper that held Wildcat's number out of Shane's wallet. It was impossible not to notice the picture of the pretty brunette behind the thin plastic protector.

Maggie Quincy had been killed in the prime of her life. She'd been a beautiful young woman with intelligent brown eyes and a stubborn chin. Rachel flipped through the other pictures. Most were of Maggie by herself, but there were a couple with both Shane and Maggie. It was obvious from the way they looked at each other that they'd been very much in love. It was ridiculous for her to think he could ever feel that strongly for anyone ever again. He'd had something very special, and part of her believed a love like that could only come along once in a lifetime.

Rachel left the car running, got out and went to the pay phone. She didn't know anything about the man she was calling or what to expect, but she called him anyway and hoped Shane knew what he was doing. The phone rang several times and she was about to hang up when a man finally answered.

"This better be important," the man said.

"Is this Jones Daugherty? Wildcat?" she asked.

"Maybe. Who the hell is this?"

This wasn't the voice of the man she'd pictured in her mind. She'd pictured Jones Daugherty as a respectable FBI agent—soft spoken, with an obvious need to help others and search for justice. Why else do the kind of work he did? No, this guy sounded like he chewed nails regularly and stomped innocent victims into the ground just for laughs.

"This is Rachel Valentine. Shane told me to call you."

"What's wrong?"

"He's been shot in the shoulder and I think he's got a concussion. He refuses to go to a hospital, and he told me to tell you we need a safe house that's close by. The idiot. He thinks he's Superman."

Wildcat laughed at that. "Don't we all. He's suffered from worse than a puny gunshot in the shoulder, and his head's as hard as a rock. I'd be surprised if he didn't crack the pavement. If he tells you he doesn't need a hospital then he doesn't."

"I'm getting a little tired of the testosterone. Heaven forbid any of you macho men do the sensible thing."

"Honey, if you'd lived through some of the things that we have you'd do your damnedest to never do another sensible thing again. Are you at a payphone?"

Rachel sighed out a frustrated breath and gave up on trying to talk sense into them. "Yes. At a gas station in Joplin."

"Give me the number and let me call you back in five minutes. I don't know what we have available in that area."

Rachel gave him the number and he immediately hung up. She was beginning to think Jones Daugherty worked in Internal Affairs because he lacked people skills.

The phone rang exactly five minutes later and he gave her directions to a place less than half an hour away and the alarm code so they could get in.

"I'm still working on a few other things Ace asked for, but I'll head in your direction after I leave the office this afternoon. It'll be late tonight before I'm able to get there, so don't let him die. He still owes me ninety-seven dollars from a poker game two years ago. Keep the doors locked and don't go outside for anything. And stay alert."

Jones hung up without giving her a chance to say thank you. Rachel hung up the phone and went back to the car. She turned off the ignition, grabbed some cash out of Shane's wallet, locked the doors and pocketed the key. There was no way she'd make it to the place Wildcat had told her of without a map.

The inside of the service station wasn't very busy. Only a few customers stood in line and a few others milled around the store. Music played on a radio in the background and people talked softly.

She grabbed a map, a few candy bars, a bag of peanuts, a Coke for her and a bottle of water for Shane. She found a few medical supplies on the opposite aisle and picked up the items she thought Shane would need. It looked like she was going to spend the next couple of days playing Florence Nightingale.

She got in the back of the line and tapped her foot impatiently, every second seeming like a millennia. The teenager in front of her was paying for his gas in pocket change, and if she'd had the extra cash she would have paid for him. When the kid finally left and it was her turn at the counter, she laid down her items and hoped she hadn't forgotten anything. She had no idea what kind of supplies would be in the safe house—whether the refrigerator would be stocked or if there'd be sheets on the bed. Beds, she corrected. She couldn't spend another night sharing a bed with Shane Quincy. It was torture at its finest.

The radio announcer picked that moment to issue an urgent bulletin.

"This information has just been released in a joint statement by the Tulsa Police Department and the FBI. The body of an unidentified man was discovered this morning with a gunshot to the head. An eyewitness claims two people are responsible for the death, and that they drove away in a tan sedan heading northwest. The witness believes one of the suspects was severely injured in the shootout, and the police corroborated the theory as they found blood other than the victim's at the scene. The police have issued arrest warrants for Shane Quincy of Louisiana and Rachel Valentine of Illinois, and both are to be considered armed and dangerous. The FBI believes these two individuals are also responsible for the death of Galen Marsh, a high profile attorney who once unsuccessfully tried to put Dominic Valentine behind bars."

Rachel kept her head down, not making eye contact with the man behind the counter, but she noticed he paused to look at her as he began to check out the rolls of gauze and first aid items. She'd never stopped to think that she was wearing Shane's blood on her shirt. Her appearance hadn't occurred to her once since she'd left Tulsa, and now she'd as good as advertised that she was a wanted criminal to a room full of people.

The radio announcer went on to explain her connection with the Valentine "mob family," and how she'd been thought to have disappeared with her father eight months before. No one knew for sure if they'd gone underground or if they were dead.

Rachel counted out money and was relieved to see she had just enough. She grabbed the bag off the counter, mumbled a hurried "Thank you" and went out the door, feeling like everyone in the store had been staring at her. And when she glanced behind her it was obvious they had been.

She kept her head down on the way back to the car but used her peripheral vision to look and see if anyone in the parking lot was overly interested in her. The Volvo came into sight, and she hit the remote to unlock the doors, sliding into the seat and then immediately locking them again.

Shane was still asleep in the backseat, but he was roused awake as she started the engine.

"Did you call him?" he asked groggily.

"Yeah." Rachel looked both ways and then sped out of the parking lot. She had a feeling their good fortune was quickly running out.

"Where are we headed?" Shane asked.

"To a little town called Alba. Your friend will meet us there tonight to make sure you're still alive. Don't move around back there. I don't want you to reopen the wound on your shoulder," she said navigating the turns. "How are you feeling?"

"Bastard of a headache. Otherwise, I've felt

worse."

Rachel dug around in the sack of supplies she'd just bought and handed him a bottle of aspirin and the water. He swallowed three pills and drank half the water and then poured the rest over his shoulder so he could see the damage.

"It's not as bad as it looks. It's a clean wound," he said.

"I bought some supplies back at the gas station and found out some interesting news."

"Yeah?" Shane said. "Like what?"

"Like we have warrants out for our arrest. It was on the radio."

"I'm sure the cops down in New Orleans are getting a kick out of that information. I'll be hearing jokes for months when this is over."

"I'm glad you can stay focused on the important things," she said, rolling her eyes.

They were headed down Highway 43 past the Joplin Airport when a black sedan pulled out in front of them.

CHAPTER NINE

Rachel hit the brakes and swerved. The tires squealed and the smell of burnt rubber filled the air. She heard Shane mumble a curse as he was jarred against the car door, and she braced herself for impact as the guardrail loomed before them. The crunch of metal was grating as the front of the Volvo glanced off the rail. There was a shatter of glass and then all was silent.

Her breathing was heavy and her hands gripped the wheel in a white-knuckled grasp. She wasn't hurt, and the crash hadn't been bad enough to deploy the airbags. She was just shocked.

"Are you okay," she asked Shane.

"Dandy." Shane moved into a sitting position so he could see the other vehicle.

The black sedan was pulled across the road so they were blocked in, and the windows were tinted so the inside couldn't be seen. Cars honked as they drove around the black sedan and traffic was beginning to pile up behind them.

"We need to get out of here," Shane said urgently.

"Where am I supposed to go? We're blocked in."

"I don't know, but the guy in front of us has reinforcements coming."

Rachel looked out the back window and saw a sedan identical to the one parked in front of them driving up the shoulder of the road and parking behind them.

"What should I do?" she asked.

Two doors opened from the black sedan and legs emerged. The driver was tall and dressed in black. His bald head was bare in the cooling weather and dark glasses covered his eyes. His top coat was unbuttoned and he held a gun down at his side. The man from the passenger side was shorter and stockier but dressed nearly the same, including the gun.

"Floor it," Shane yelled.

"Oh, man," Rachel said, putting the car in reverse and moving away from the guard rail with a squeal of tires. "Hold on tight." She put the car in drive and punched the gas pedal to the floor. The tires spun and smoke rose from the pavement, but then the car took off like a shot. She headed straight for the black sedan and said every prayer she knew as the men raised their guns.

Both men dived out of the way as the Volvo hit the side end of the car. There was a crunch of fiberglass and the black sedan was pushed aside. Rachel jerked against her seatbelt and hit her head on the drivers' side window. A gunshot shattered the back window and she ducked low in her seat.

"Take the off-ramp to the airport. The guys in the other car are getting closer," Shane said and Rachel turned the wheel just in time to take the exit.

Rachel weaved through traffic with the pedal mashed to the floor, but the guys following them still gained ground. "What are you doing?" she asked as Shane folded down the back seat so he could reach into the trunk.

"I'm seeing if the previous owner of this car had anything that might be useful in a situation like this one."

Rachel felt like an idiot. She'd never thought to check the trunk when they'd been stopped at the gas station.

"And bingo," Shane said.

Rachel kept one eye on the road and the other on Shane as he pulled a hard-shell black suitcase out of the trunk and opened the lid. He had a rifle put together almost before she could blink.

"Umm, Shane," she said nervously, looking at what was coming up.

"A little busy right now, Sugar. Just keep driving."

"Tollbooth," she said softly.

"What?"

"There's a freaking tollbooth in front of us!" she screamed, "and I'm a little short on change right now."

"You'll just have to wing it. Try to keep the car in a straight line. No sudden movements," he ordered.

Rachel was beginning to miss the concussed Shane who couldn't open his mouth. She growled low in her throat and kept the pedal pressed to the floor. The booths were all manned and the gates were slowly letting people through the line. She found a lane with no cars and did as Shane said.

He grunted as he lifted the rifle so it was propped on the back of the seat. His shoulder was bleeding again, and she knew he had to be in a tremendous amount of pain. If they got out of this alive, she swore she'd play Florence Nightingale without any complaints. She'd even get rid of the little ones inside her head.

"What are you waiting for?" she asked as the gate got closer. Panic and fear rose in her throat, but she kept driving, both hands steady on the wheel. A man stuck his head out of the tollbooth and waved his arms, gesturing for her to slow down. But when she didn't comply he opened the back door of the booth and ran away. Rachel didn't blame him. She wanted to run away, too.

She squeezed her eyes shut at the last second and they crashed through the gate. Cars swerved and horns blared, but she kept the car moving forward in a straight line. The black car was through the gate seconds behind them. She heard two pops from the rifle in Shane's hands and the squeal of breaks. The black car's tires blew out and it flipped into the air, rolling across four lanes of traffic.

Rachel let out the breath she'd been holding.

"Right there," Shane said, pointing to a parking garage. "That's long term parking. We'll make a quick car switch and get out of here. We've got to get back to the main road before they get smart enough to close all the airport exits. It'll take them at least another ten minutes to get things organized. The police don't have the authority to shut down the airport. It has to go through federal channels."

Rachel pulled into the long term parking lot and into the first empty spot she came across.

"Dammit, Shane, let me help you get out," she said as he tried to maneuver out of the car by himself.

"I can take care of myself. Pop the trunk and get whatever's in there while I find a car."

Rachel blew out a breath in frustration and did as he said. There'd be plenty of time to argue with the stubborn man later. She gathered a couple of duffle bags that were in the trunk and stood by, silently arguing with herself, as Shane struggled to stand upright and pick the lock on an old Honda Civic.

The car door opened and Shane slid behind the wheel, his hands clumsy as he took the plastic off the underside of the wheel and stripped the wires. Rachel threw the bags in the backseat and waited outside the car until she heard the purr of the engine.

"Don't even think about driving," she said. "You wouldn't make it down the block."

Shane scooted across to the passenger side and leaned his head back against the seat. He closed his eyes for a second and caught his breath. Sweat beaded on his brow and his hair was damp with perspiration. His skin was pale and his breathing labored.

Rachel pulled the stolen car back out to the main road and was glad to see Shane had been right about the authorities not being organized enough to shut down the airport in a timely manner. Too much red tape. God Bless it.

"Give me the map," Shane said. "I'll see if I can find a back road to get us to the safe house. The less visible we are the better."

Shane navigated her down one lane, dirt roads and what looked like cow pastures. She never would have found her way to the little town without his help. It was barely a spec on the map with a total population of less than five hundred.

"There it is. County Lane 245," Shane said, pointing out the window to a wheat field.

"There what is?" Rachel asked. "There's nothing out there."

"Look at the fence and tell me there's nothing out there."

Rachel looked at the expensive iron fence that was weaved with barbed wire and thought Shane might have a point. She pulled the car onto a dirt drive and stopped at the gate. An electric keypad sat off to one side, so she rolled down her window and entered the code Jones had given her, keeping her fingers crossed that it worked and a team of FBI agents wasn't about to swoop down on them.

The gate opened slowly in front of her and she drove the car through. She needed a shower, a hot meal and a big glass of wine. Rachel looked over at

Shane and saw he was slumped forward, only his seatbelt keeping him upright. She reached over and touched his forehead. He was burning with fever and his face was flushed. The other things could wait. Shane was her first priority. If only she could find the damn house.

Rachel drove down the dirt path for more than a mile before seeing anything other than waist-high grass and wheat. A big red barn came into view, and it looked to be in bad shape. Windows were broken and wood had rotted away, leaving holes large enough for a horse to walk through. But the dirt road continued around the side of the barn, so she kept following it and ended up inside the barn itself.

She was in a garage of some sort and there was a perfectly sturdy looking wall right in front of her. There was a thick metal door with no doorknob and a keypad similar to the one at the front gate next to it. It looked like the old barn was just a cover for the real safe house. She put the car in reverse and pulled out of the garage, turning the car around so she could back it in—just in case they needed to make a quick getaway. She'd learned that little trick early on in her attempts at running away.

She assumed the keypad used the same entry code as the front gate and typed it in. A little green light flashed above the door and she heard the snick of a lock. She pushed open the door, unsure of what she'd find waiting for her on the inside, considering what the outside looked like.

It was a small space, but it was clean and there were no holes in the walls. After staying at Jake's otel almost anything would be an upgrade, but this was very nice. She went back to the car and tried to wake Shane. He mumbled something incoherent under his breath but didn't open his eyes.

"Come on, tough guy. I need your help here," she said as she moved under his arm and tried to pull him out of the car. The man was solid muscle and had a good hundred pounds on her.

"I knew you wouldn't be able to resist me," he said, nuzzling her neck.

"Yeah, you're a real catch right now."

He stumbled against her as she walked him into the house and closed the metal door with her foot. She led him into one of the two bedrooms and laid him down gently on the bed. He was burning with fever and hot to the touch. She had to get him out of his clothes and cool him down. And then she had to figure out what to do about the wound in his shoulder.

Rachel turned to get the bag of supplies out of the car, but a strong grip around her wrist stopped her in her tracks. Shane pulled her down so she was sprawled on top of him.

"Don't leave," he said. "It's too dangerous."

His grip was powerful, bruising, and it amazed

her how much strength he had even in the condition he was in.

She tried to soothe him as best she could. He was getting agitated and tossing and turning on the bed, no doubt because of the fever.

"I'm not leaving. I just need to get a few things to make you feel better."

"Promise me," he said, increasing his grip till she yelped at the sting. "Everyone I love is always leaving me. Can't take it anymore. Hurts too bad."

Rachel assured herself that he didn't know what was saying, but it was still a nice feeling for him to believe he loved her. "I promise I won't leave you." She bent her head and kissed him softly on the cheek.

Rachel ran and got the bags out of the car and dropped them in the dining room. Wildcat's instructions rang in her head, and after the day they'd just had she didn't want to take any chances, so she double checked the door locks and looked around the house for an alternate way to enter. Or exit.

The place was very plain, laid out like a small two bedroom apartment. The floor and walls were beige, as were the countertops and bathroom fixtures. She didn't find any other doors or windows in the house. There was only one way in and one way out as far as she could see, and claustrophobia wound its way around her. Having an alternate route of escape had been a habit since she'd first disappeared, and she hated the feeling of being trapped.

Rachel riffled through the drawers and cabinets until she found the things she needed for Shane—scissors and plenty of towels and rags. She carried the bags of supplies into the bedroom along with a large bowl of water. It was time to get down to business and get Shane back on his feet. She could freely admit now that she needed him to help her get out of this mess alive.

"Okay," she said, preparing herself. "We've got to get those clothes off." She held the scissors in her hand and looked nervously at the man lying before her. "Suck it up, Rachel. You've seen a naked man before." But her subconscious was telling her she'd never seen a naked man like Shane Quincy before. And she knew her subconscious was right.

Rachel cut away his shirt and winced as she pulled it away from the wound at his shoulder. The blood had caused the shirt to stick to the skin and she had to soak it with water before it would come free. She pulled off his socks and shoes and tackled the button of his jeans. His chest and stomach were hard with muscle and a fine sprinkling of dark hair covered his chest and trailed its way down below the waistband of his jeans. Rachel chewed on her lip nervously and tugged at the denim at his hips. And when she finally pulled them off and got a good look at Shane Quincy in all his glory, she was pretty sure he wasn't the only one who was burning with fever.

"Maggie," he called out, thrashing around on the bed, his sweat-soaked body already dampening the sheets. "Maggie!" His demands for his dead wife grew stronger the higher his fever went, and Rachel felt tears sting her eyes at his obvious pain.

"Ssh, it'll be okay," she soothed. "I'm here with you, and nothing bad is going to happen."

"Rachel?" he whispered.

"That's right. It's Rachel." She bathed him with cool water and cleaned the wound at his shoulder. He was right that it wasn't so bad. There was only a small entry and exit wound, and the area didn't seem to be infected. She applied some salve and wrapped it in bandages.

It was the knot on his head that looked bad. A lump the size of an egg protruded into a starburst of color. She'd read somewhere that a person needing to stay awake while they had a concussion was just a myth, but she wasn't sure. She tried to wake him and get him to swallow more pain killers, but he was all the way out.

It was well after dark by the time she'd finished seeing to Shane's comfort. She took a quick shower, heated a bowl of soup and ate standing over the sink while watching the clock on the wall. It was ten o'clock and Jones Daugherty still hadn't shown up. Was it just a coincidence that the men in the black cars had found them so soon after she'd talked to Wildcat? She couldn't be sure, and she didn't know what Wildcat's absence meant, but the gnawing in her stomach told her it couldn't be good. She was beginning to think Shane needed to think twice about who he could trust.

Rachel checked the door and made sure the code was set before turning off the lights and climbing into bed next to Shane. He was still as death, and Rachel wondered if he'd remember the promise she'd given him to never leave him. She curled up next to him and tried not to think about the day she'd have to break that promise.

CHAPTER TEN

Two days and nights passed, and there was still no change in Shane's condition.

Rachel's nerves strung tighter the longer time went on and no word came from Jones Daugherty. She found herself jumping at every creak and shadow, and the safe house was starting to feel like a prison instead of a haven. The duffle bags that had belonged to the shooter in Tulsa were full of guns and cash, and she made sure each weapon was loaded and put in a spot she could reach easily.

The wound in Shane's shoulder was healing nicely, but the fever hadn't gone away. He woke in fits and starts, and his body was restless on the bed. His speech was jumbled and incomprehensible, except for the times he'd called out for Maggie. It was Maggie he saw in his fevered state, and he'd begged her forgiveness repeatedly. Rachel tried not to let the slip hurt her, but it had. Because she could never be the woman he really wanted.

His nightmares hadn't stopped just because of his injuries, but now he was trapped in them, caught somewhere between the past and the present, and the torture only stopped when the final scene had played out. It destroyed her to see his torment over and over again, and she was helpless to stop it.

Rachel did her best to cool his fevered body off with damp rags, but his skin was hot to the touch and seemed to grow hotter as the hours passed. She whispered assurances in his ear as he thrashed about on the bed and held him down when his struggles loosened the bandages over his shoulder. She'd had little luck getting medicine or soup down his throat, but the few times he'd woken she'd cajoled, begged or forced them down. She went to bed each night feeling as if she'd fought a battle. And lost.

Shane drifted awake slowly, his mind disoriented and his body aching. Something wasn't right, but he couldn't put his finger on what it was exactly. He took stock of his body, cataloguing the stiffness in his shoulder and the nagging headache just behind his eyes. He stretched his sore muscles slowly, and cool sheets shifted around his naked body. And as he moved something soft and warm pressed up against him.

He'd know the feel of her anywhere. The scent of her. She was unique in every way, and he was beginning to get used to the way his body hardened every time she was near. But why was Rachel in bed with him, and where were they? What had they done? And why couldn't he remember?

She was pressed close enough to him so he could feel every curve of her body. He drew her closer and she tangled her legs with his in sleep. Her skin was silky smooth and her hair fell softly over his chest. Her breathing was slow and steady, and he found it sweet the way she snuggled into him, as if she needed him to sleep peacefully.

His body woke much faster than his mind. Sleep and confusion still clung to him and his instincts took over. He ran his hand down her back, past her hip and thigh and then back up again, marveling at the different textures of the soft cotton shirt and silky panties she slept in to the smooth expanse of skin. She sighed and her breath feathered his skin, hardening him to the point of madness, and her hands moved over the bare skin of his abdomen. She was temptation and desire, every forbidden pleasure he could think of wrapped into one. He sucked in a breath and knew he had to have her, wondered why he'd waited so long.

Rachel was branded in his mind, on his skin. His name escaped her lips and he was trapped in her spell. Shane couldn't help but lower his lips and gently kiss her cheeks, her chin, her lips. His hands found their way under the shirt she wore and skimmed over the soft mounds of her breasts, rubbing across her sensitive nipples, causing her to moan and shift restlessly against him.

She murmured sweet sounds of want and need into his mouth as her hands became more aggressive. He rolled so she was pinned beneath him, and he had no conscious thought of removing the shirt or filmy scrap of lace at the juncture of her thighs. He only knew that they were finally skin to skin. Shane wondered fleetingly if it was all a dream and hoped he'd never wake if it was true. It was just the two of them, brought together in an unknown time and place. There was no danger or reckless chances. Just a man and a woman lost in each other. Made for each other.

Rachel moaned as his lips found her breast and desire roared through him. Her breath was faster now, and he knew if there'd been light in the room her gaze would have been locked on his, filled with the same longing he knew was in his own. He needed her. Needed to possess her, needed her to chase away the demons of his past.

Her fingers pressed into the flesh of his back and her legs scissored around him, so they were locked heat to heat, heart to heart. She arched against him in desperation, and the shaky control he had over his body snapped.

His mouth clamped to hers. Tongues mated and

passions raged. And then he was inside her, and he wondered how he could have ever been any place else. She clamped around him tightly and screamed out in ecstasy. Her moist heat pulsed around him and the sensation was more than he could bear. He buried his face against her neck and whispered her name as he found fulfillment.

It was her name he whispered. And no one else's.

Rachel opened her eyes but only saw darkness. Her skin was damp and cooling and tears ran down her cheeks. She wasn't sure why other than the fact that making love with Shane had been the most beautiful experience of her life. The problem was it had probably been nothing more than simply satisfying the body to him.

Shane's body was still heavy on hers, his breathing erratic and his skin heated. Their hearts thumped in time and she could still taste him on her lips. She'd never felt more attuned to anyone. Or more alone.

But she couldn't enjoy the afterglow of their lovemaking. Her mind kept screaming she'd made a terrible mistake. Questions of doubt bombarded her. How could she have let this happen? Didn't he know how much he could hurt her? Did he even care? Apparently he had no problems making love to another woman when he was still in love with his dead wife. She'd been called Maggie enough in the last two days to feel a bitter jealousy toward a woman she hadn't even known.

Anger began to simmer low in her gut and the tears dried quickly. She knew she was as much to blame as he was, but that didn't stop the act from hurting any less. She wasn't made for one-night stands or quick flings, and Shane wasn't good for anything but.

She pushed at his shoulders and he rolled to the side. He reached for her and tried to pull her in his arms, but she sat up quickly and pulled the sheet around her, covering her nakedness and shame.

"What's wrong?" he asked, searching for and flipping on the lamp on the bedside table.

She blinked at the brightness of the light and wished she were back in darkness. Shane laid beside her, his body a masterpiece of perfection and the lazy smile on his face smug and content.

"What's wrong? What's wrong!" she shouted. "How could you do this to me?"

"Well, if you need me to explain the particulars I'd be glad to, but I'd just as soon show you again, Sugar." He smiled and eyed the sheet wrapped loosely around her breasts, giving it a gentle tug. She held fast to the sheet and what was left of her pride and jumped from the bed to face him standing up.

“This isn’t a joke. You took advantage of the situation. You knew I didn’t want to sleep with you,” she said.

“Well, it was a little hard to figure out the signals, considering I woke up naked in bed with you and you were wrapped around me tighter than a glove. It’s not as if I got shot on purpose just so I could have my wicked way with you.”

“I was taking care of you, you ungrateful—” she couldn’t even finish the sentence she was so angry. “I was asleep,” she finally said.

“So was I. And it’s not as if you were fighting me off. What’s this really about, Rachel?”

“Let me make this as plain as possible. I will not be a substitute for your wife. I’m not her. I never will be, and I wouldn’t be if I could. I don’t sleep with men I hardly know, and I sure as hell don’t sleep with men who are just looking for an easy lay until they can move on to the next available woman. I need more than just a roll in the sheets to be satisfied.”

Shane’s face grew dark and angry at her words. “Correct me if I’m wrong, Sugar, but it was your name I called out at the end.”

He rubbed his hands through his hair in frustration and stood up to face her, unmindful of his nakedness or how it was distracting her from the conversation.

"I've never compared you to Maggie. Where the hell is that coming from? And whoever said anything about you being easy. Right now you're being a definite pain in the ass. I'm not a mind reader. You can't keep your hands off me one minute and the next you don't want anything to do with me. Just what exactly is it that you do want?"

"I want to get out of this mess alive. And if you'd prefer not to see things through to the end due to our current situation, we can certainly terminate our business arrangement. But if we do go on together, I want you to keep your hands to yourself. I have enough problems in my life right now."

"Understood, Sugar. But maybe you should sleep in your own bed from now on just to make sure."

Shane turned around and walked into the bathroom, slamming the door behind him. She heard the shower turn on and went into the other bedroom to put on clothes and get herself together. It didn't seem to matter what she did or how she tried to protect herself. It looked like Shane Quincy was going to break her heart anyway.

Shane leaned his head against the cold tile of the shower and wished he knew what the hell had just happened. He tried to think back over the last couple of days, but the hours seemed to run together. He vaguely remembered Rachel always being there when his eyes had opened, shoving pills and food down his throat and going back and forth between pleading and arguing with him to get better and wake up.

Well, he was awake now, and he wished he could crawl back under the covers. Only now that he knew what it felt like to make love to Rachel, he wanted her to be under the covers with him. Forever. And that scared the hell out of him because he wasn't sure if he believed in forever anymore. He knew better than anyone how temporary, and how fragile, life was.

He had no idea why Rachel would think he was comparing her to Maggie. Maggie was gone. She would always be a part of him, but she was his past. Rachel was his future. Or at least he wanted her to be. From the way she'd reacted after they'd made love things weren't looking too hopeful.

The hot water pounded on his sore muscles, and he didn't care about the bandage at his shoulder getting wet or that the water stung the raw knot at his temple. At least he was alive. The amount of pain rioting through his body told him that much. He wanted to feel whole again, and right now he just felt tired and defeated. Some bodyguard he was. He'd spent God knows how long in unconsciousness while his charge had gone unprotected. Anything could have happened to Rachel while he'd been down. And he refused to be responsible for the death of anyone else he loved.

Love. The word in itself was frightening, and he found himself backtracking, thinking of another way to describe his feelings for Rachel. He wasn't ready to love, especially after knowing her for such a short time. Surely a few days couldn't determine a lifetime. Besides, he wasn't capable of loving anyone again. And it wasn't fair to give Rachel anything less. No wonder she was angry with him. It was obvious she'd already thought through the consequences of how things would be between them if they took their attraction too far. He'd already told her he would never give all of himself to a woman again. And she'd taken the words inspired by his nightmares to heart. He only had himself to blame for saying something so stupid. So hurtful.

Shane soaped up and rinsed off quickly, the layers of sweat and sickness swirling down the drain along with the despair he felt. He could fix things with Rachel, but they had to get out of their current situation. She was right about having more than enough to deal with at the moment.

He turned off the water and got out on shaky legs. He needed food and something to help the headache he couldn't remember not having. It was time to take back control of the situation. He wrapped a towel loosely around his hips and walked back into the bedroom.

He heard Rachel moving around in the kitchen

and decided from the way she was banging pots and pans around that her mood hadn't improved. It was probably best to give them both a little space for the time being. She needed to cool off and he needed to come up with a plan.

The sheets had been stripped off the bed and a washing machine rumbled from somewhere in the house. It looked like Rachel was anxious to get rid of any memory of what they'd done. It was fine with him. He'd made her a promise and he wasn't about to go back on it, no matter how much he still ached with wanting her.

He found his jeans folded on the dresser. They'd been washed, but holes had been torn in both knees from his fall. A stack of new shirts sat folded in the drawer in several different sizes along with white athletic socks and a package of underwear. He dressed and did nothing more than towel dry his wet hair and gave a cursory thought to shaving when he rubbed his hand across the stubble on his face. The idea was quickly dismissed as the smell of something hot reached his nose.

His system was off and he had no idea what time it was. The clock on the microwave said six, but he wasn't sure if it was A.M. or P.M. Rachel had sandwiches and soup sitting on the table when he came into the room. Her dark hair was pulled back into a knot at the base of her neck and thin wisps of hair had slipped free. Her face was flushed and there were dark circles under her eyes. Obviously he'd given her more than one sleepless night.

"I didn't thank you for taking care of me," he said as he sat at the table. Things were awkward between them, but he tried his best to put her at ease. They had a difficult road ahead of them and they needed to be able to communicate. "I know I'm not usually the easiest patient."

She kept her head down and wouldn't look him in the eye. "You would have done the same for me. I just hope you're not overdoing it too soon."

"I know my limits. I'm feeling better. Just a little stiffness in my shoulder, and I'll have to watch accidentally opening the wound since I wasn't able to get stitches. It might still come to that."

"As long as I don't have to give them to you." She sat down across from him and picked at her food. He'd already inhaled his and was on a second helping. Her brow was furrowed and she shifted in her chair. He could tell she had something important on her mind.

"We need to decide how long we're staying here," she finally said. "I'm beginning to go stir crazy, and I'm anxious to get to Chicago, get the list, and hand it over. I know the way Angelo works, and Galen Marsh's death will be just the beginning if we don't see this through as quickly as possible. I don't like being in limbo like this, out here in the middle of nowhere while innocent people are being slaughtered."

"What did Wildcat say when you talked to him?"

"Your pal Wildcat never bothered to show up." The frustration was palpable in her voice. "There's no phone in this place, and I left the disposable cells in the car. Wildcat gave me explicit instructions not to leave the house, and I've spent three days staring at beige walls. For all I know, Wildcat could be sitting outside with either a group of FBI agents or some of Angelo's men. I'm not too anxious to find out which one."

"If Wildcat didn't show up, it's for a good reason. He wouldn't take the chance of leading anyone to us accidentally."

"If you say so, but you mentioned the last time you talked to him that you were sorry you hadn't kept in contact with him over the last couple of years. Two years is a long time, and people can change."

"Not Wildcat. He's as solid as they come. You've just got to trust me on this one."

"Fine. I guess I don't have any choice, but it doesn't make me feel very safe to know we're locked in here like prisoners with only one way to escape. What were they thinking putting one metal door and no windows in this place? It's enough to drive a person insane."

Rachel tore her sandwich apart in what he

recognized as a nervous gesture. She was scared, and the last couple of days were starting to take their toll. He hadn't stopped to consider what she must be feeling. Most civilians he knew would have reached their breaking point long ago. He'd taken her strength for granted and forgotten that she'd lost a father, her home and most likely her friends. He'd let her ramble on and get everything off her chest, and then he was going to suggest she take a nice long soak in the tub and get a solid eight hours of sleep.

"Of course, they could try to burn us out," she continued. "Though I'd hate to think that they'd try the same old, tired routine. I know dad always had a fondness for keeping people off guard. It was one of his trademarks."

This was information Shane already knew. The last thing he wanted to get into was a conversation about Dominic Valentine. He rinsed his dishes out in the sink and put them in the drain pan to dry. Rachel continued to sit at the table and stare at her untouched food, so he took the liberty of clearing her plate from in front of her and tidying up.

He knew she wouldn't welcome it, but he needed to touch her. To reassure her that everything would be okay. He walked up behind her and put his hands on the back of her neck, ignoring the way she jumped skittishly at his touch. Then he kneaded the knotted muscles slowly until she all but melted beneath him.

"It wouldn't be very practical for a safe house to

have only one route of escape," he said, continuing the massage for a few more minutes. "Come on, I'll show you."

Shane took her hand and held it casually as he led her into the second bedroom. He opened the closet door and moved a wooden shelf out of the way. Behind it was a square, no bigger than a suitcase, with a sliding door. "There's your second doorway," Shane said, sliding it open.

It was dark inside and smelled of earth and disuse. Cobwebs clung to the corners.

"Where does it lead?" she asked.

"I don't know, but it'll open up into a bigger tunnel and go for a couple of miles. It's standard for any FBI safe house. But if you have to use it make sure you take a flashlight." He closed the door and moved the shelf back in place.

Shane went into the small living room and looked at the arsenal of weapons she had laid out. "Looks like you were prepared for anything."

"I figured I had enough firepower to scare anybody who tried to come through that door," she said. "Of course now that I know about door number two, I think I'll opt to take the coward's way out."

"I've never known anyone who was less of a coward than you," Shane said. He picked up a .9mm Glock and checked to make sure it was fully loaded.

He slipped it in the small of his back and headed to the metal door that led to the outside.

"Wait a minute. Where are you going?" Rachel asked.

"I'm going to take a look around the grounds and make sure we're secure. I want you to stay here."

"Like hell. I want out of this place. And what if you have a relapse or something while you're out there? The bump on your head looks worse than it did two days ago, not to mention how much blood you lost with the hole in your shoulder. You'll feel pretty stupid if you get out there and pass out."

"I'm fine, Sugar. Almost as good as new, but I'm glad to see you're so worried about me."

"I'm worried about me," she said with a scowl. "What if your friend turned you in and the FBI is out there waiting to arrest you? We have warrants out for our arrest."

"Huh. I'd forgotten about that," Shane said. "Make sure you use the second escape route if you hear shots." The color drained from her face and shame washed over him. He was still raw from the words she'd spoken earlier, but that was no excuse. Shane brushed a finger down the side of her cheek, but kept his face void of emotion as she jerked back from his touch. "There's no one out there, Sugar," he reassured her. "I just want to get a lay of the land and see what we're up against. If there is someone out there I'll deal with it. This is what I do. If I'm not back in an hour use the door in the closet and get as far away as you can."

Shane closed the door in the face of a very angry woman. He needed to get away and think things through. Two years was a long time, and he was starting to suspect that Rachel could be right. Jones Daugherty might not be the man he remembered.

Angelo Valentine was enraged.

The servants were still cleaning up the mess from his reaction to the messenger who'd had the unfortunate task of telling Angelo that Jimmy Grabbaldi was dead. It wasn't the fact Jimmy was dead that bothered Angelo so much. He'd been planning to dispose of Jimmy anyway. It was the fact that Jimmy had failed to kill his bitch of a niece and the man she'd brought in to help her with family business. Angelo couldn't tolerate failure. Wouldn't tolerate failure. There was incompetence all around him—the men who worked for him were easy come, easy go, but incompetent just the same. If he had to dispose of everyone who'd ever failed him, he'd have a very short payroll. How hard could it be to kill a former interior designer, for God's sake?

Angelo walked into the den and poured himself three fingers of whiskey from the decanter over the fireplace. He was expecting company shortly and preferred to have the meeting in comfort rather than his stuffy office—the stuffy office that had once belonged to his brother. Not to mention his guest might find the current state of the office in bad taste. Blood still soaked the Aubusson rug and brain matter was splattered on the walls. He'd found in the past that members of law enforcement reacted strangely to such things.

The oval mirror over the mantle showed a man distinguished in years—the silver at his temples and the lines of age on his face emphasized as much. He didn't have his brother Dom's charisma or the natural leadership that had emanated from him. But he held power just the same. He inspired loyalty in his men through fear like Dom never had. Nice guys never finished first in the mob. And Dom had too much nice in his old age. He'd gotten soft and never quite bounced back from the death of his youngest daughter.

The order of events had worked out exactly as Angelo planned, all the dominoes falling nicely into place. First, take advantage of Dom's weaknesses, meaning kill his wife and daughters, and then destroy Dom. Piece of cake.

Rachel would've already been dead if it hadn't been for Dom's harebrained scheme to turn on his business family and his rivals alike. And so Angelo had had to move things around in his timetable and dispose of Dom first. Dom's disappearance and eventual death had been easy to orchestrate—members of rival families had been glad to help out once they'd learned Dom had turned traitor. It had been even easier for the grieving brother to take over the reins of the Valentine empire. Rachel was the only loose end left.

Chimes echoed through the house and his butler opened the door. Two sets of footsteps clipped along the marble tile and there was a light rap on the heavy doors that led into the den. Angelo kept his place standing by the stone hearth—a position of power so he could look down on an underling.

"Enter," he commanded.

His visitor didn't seem impressed by the opulence of the room. And his visitor especially didn't seem impressed by the company.

"Mr. Valentine. You said you wanted to see me." The visitor smiled slightly and took a seat in one of the club chairs facing the fireplace. Angelo didn't know why, but he had the sudden feeling he was no longer the one in control.

"There's a certain place in my organization for overconfidence," Angelo said. "This is not one of those times or places. Everyone's usefulness runs out eventually. It's best you remember that."

The visitor nodded, but the small smile never vanished. Sweat snaked down Angelo's spine and dampened the Italian shirt he wore. He could smell his own fear and wondered if the visitor could as well.

"Tell me what your plans are for my niece. I don't want that list to make it out of the bank vault. Do you understand?"

"Oh, I understand, Mr. Valentine. Now it's time for you to understand that I'm the one calling the shots. I don't want any more screw ups, and your men thus far have seemed less than competent."

"And you'd better understand where the money's coming from," Angelo said. "Don't disappoint me. And one more thing. A little change from my earlier orders. I want Rachel brought to me alive. Do what you want with the man and anyone else who gets in your way, but I want Rachel to know what happened to her father before she dies. And I want her to know who's going to end it all."

It was everything Angelo could do not to rub his hands together in anticipation. Rachel had caused him considerable trouble, and it was only fair he paid her back in full. Nobody messed with Angelo Valentine, and the knife he carried in the sheath at his side would guarantee it was the last thing Rachel would ever remember.

"Whatever you want, Mr. Valentine," the visitor said, smirking. "But a kidnapping is going to make my price go up by a hundred thousand."

"Or I could kill you now, and find someone else who is more accommodating," Angelo countered.

"You could certainly try." The visitor got up from the chair and walked away calmly, the small smile never wavering.

Angelo didn't take a breath until the front door closed.

CHAPTER ELEVEN

Dawn was just breaking over the horizon when Shane stepped out of the house.

Gravel crunched beneath his feet and he looked the stolen Honda over thoroughly to make sure no one had tampered with it. He grabbed one of the disposable cell phone out of the front seat and a look at the screen told him Wildcat hadn't tried to call. Not good news. He shoved the phone in his back pocket and left the protection of the garage area. If there was going to be a showdown, he wanted to be prepared and take every advantage of the land and any resources at his disposal.

Unfortunately, the land they were stuck on had a whole lot of nothing, and there were no resources that he could see in any direction. The dilapidated barn sat in the middle of acres of six-foot high wheat. Trees were nonexistent and there were no houses.

Shane figured they'd been lucky up to this point. If Wildcat had turned against them their chances for survival had decreased significantly, and it was a danger to stay in one place too long. His old commander was brilliant at combat tactics, but Shane still held hope that his friend would come through for them in the end. Old habits were hard to break.

Shane had used up more than half of the hour he'd given Rachel as a time gauge. He'd had enough time to think of a plan, but there were a lot of things that could still go wrong. There were too many variables that factored into keeping Rachel safe, and he wasn't afraid to admit he was being overly cautious where she was concerned. Maybe he'd lost his edge since Maggie's death. He'd been stuck behind a desk for two years looking for missing persons and tracking down people who were defrauding their insurance companies.

This was not the time to lose confidence in his abilities now that Rachel's life was on the line, he thought.

He headed back toward the house and Rachel when he felt the vibrations under his feet. A black SUV, windows tinted black and dirt flying from under its tires, came up behind him. Shane had the gun in his hand in an instant and hunkered down in the tall stalks of wheat, training the weapon on whoever was about to get out of the vehicle.

The passenger side door opened and a pair of

denim clad legs stepped out. The woman was petite and her blond hair grazed just above her shoulders, framing an elfin face. Shane would have thought she looked like a perky high school cheerleader if hadn't been for her eyes. She had cop eyes, intense and assessing as she looked around the area for possible threats. She wore a shoulder holster over a casual white t-shirt and thick-soled Vibram boots under a pair of baggy jeans. He had her pegged for a Fed, despite the government license plates on the SUV or the casual clothing.

It was the driver of the SUV who finally pulled Shane's curiosity away from the woman. Jones Daugherty walked around the back of the vehicle and joined his companion. Jones had always been a big man, but he seemed like a giant next to the petite woman, and it looked like he'd been hitting the gym hard over the last couple of years. Other than being a little thicker across the chest, he still looked the same—the same blond hair cropped close to the skull in a military style and the same intricate tattoo that ran from his wrist to his elbow.

But there was definitely one noticeable difference. Shane had never seen Wildcat squeeze a colleague on the ass and whisper a suggestion lewd enough to make the colleague in question blush.

"Come on out, Ace," Wildcat called out. "I know you're out there somewhere. I can feel you staring at me. We need to talk."

Shane wasn't really left with any other options. Wildcat was standing between him and Rachel, and his first priority was keeping her safe. Shane stood up slowly and left his hiding place, keeping his weapon trained on the enemy. The action left a bitter taste in his mouth since it was his closest friend at the other end of the target.

Jones met Shane's steady gaze and glanced at the gun in his hand, laughing a little at the sight. He held his hands up in a sign of surrender. "Don't shoot, Ace. Though I probably shouldn't be worried about you hitting me since you've been playing private eye for the last couple of years. I bet you've lost all your instincts, spying on cheating wives and looking for lost kittens."

"Like hell, I have," Shane said indignantly, wishing he hadn't had the same thought mere minutes before. "Any time you want to go a round just say the word. Who's your friend?"

"We'll get to that. I figure I should start out by telling you I got trapped in Chicago for a couple of days," Wildcat said. "It's a real mess up there, and I couldn't leave in the middle of it without drawing suspicion my way. People have a tendency to keep an eye on IA men since we're considered the bad guys. And the lady you're pointing the gun at is my fiancée. She's a lot meaner than I am, and she'll get real nasty if you shoot me. I've already been fitted for my tux."

“Special Agent Carrie Layne,” she said, nodding in his direction and giving him a smile meant to put him at ease. “I’ve heard a lot about you. And most of it was fairly entertaining. Maybe you could show me the tattoo you got in Afghanistan some time.”

“Geez, Wildcat. You told her about that,” Shane said, feeling the heat rush to his cheeks.

“There are no secrets between us. Which means your secrets aren’t safe either,” Jones said, putting an arm around Carrie’s shoulders.

Shane signed and lowered the gun. “Maybe we should go inside and talk about this.”

Rachel heard the beeps that signified someone was trying to get through the metal door. She didn’t want to take the chance that it wasn’t Shane, so she grabbed a sawed off shotgun from her stash and pointed it at the door.

The door opened and a huge man filled the entryway. He was taller and more muscled than Shane, which wasn’t an easy feat, and she figured the man could have passed as a fighter in the UFC. Or maybe even the Incredible Hulk. She pumped the shotgun before he could get a foot over the threshold.

“Whoa, honey,” Wildcat said. “Let’s not jump to conclusions.”

The giant of a man stepped to the side and revealed a tiny blond woman, but Rachel looked over her head to the man behind. She breathed a sigh of relief when she saw Shane rounding up the trio. He seemed unharmed and unconcerned about the strangers who had invaded their sanctuary.

"It's okay, Rachel," Shane said. "I'd like you to meet Jones Daugherty and his fiancée, Carrie Layne."

Rachel looked at the man square in the eyes and didn't bother to put down the shotgun. "You're late, Agent Daugherty. Have you come to help us or did you spend the last two days setting up a way to trap us here?"

"Are you always this suspicious?" Wildcat asked and took a seat at the kitchen table.

"You could say I've learned to be cautious over the years," she answered.

"I have to say I'm curious to know the answer as well," Shane said. "Especially after I've gone to all the trouble to assure Rachel that you're the most trustworthy friend I have. Now would be a hell of a time to be wrong about that."

"I assure you, Shane, that Jones has had nothing but your best interests at heart since you called him," Carrie said defensively. She gave Shane a hard look and squeezed her lover's hand in a reassuring gesture.

"Put the gun away, Rachel," Shane said as he nodded to the woman his best friend had chosen to spend the rest of his life with. "Let's all sit down and talk this out."

Rachel put down the shotgun and took the chair next to Shane. He lounged like he hadn't a care in the world, and she tried to emulate him. The lack of sleep over the past couple of days was beginning to catch up with her, and she found all she wanted to do was climb back into bed.

"I brought the files on the agents you asked for," Jones began and handed over a folder at least three inches thick of papers.

Rachel gave Shane a curious look and waited for him to explain.

"We've already determined that someone in the FBI has been feeding information to Angelo," Shane said. "And more than likely that same agent is responsible for your father's disappearance and the murder of Agent Culver, since only an inside person would know when and where Culver and Dom were meeting. I want you to look through the files of these agents and see if anyone looks familiar to you."

He handed her the file and she flipped back the blue cover with the confidential seal stamped across it. "This could take awhile. I had no idea so many agents had worked on trying to catch my father or any of his men."

"These agents are from all over the country," Shane said. "Not just Chicago. Your father had interests in several states."

Rachel began flipping through the pages and Shane turned his attention toward Agent Layne. "How do you fit in here?" he asked. "Are you IA like Jones or do you have a personal interest in the Valentine case?"

"I've never been assigned to any of the Valentine task forces directly," Carrie said. "I work in the Violent Crimes Unit, so sometimes my cases overlap with the guys in Organized Crime."

"Not many agents would be willing to risk their career for people they've never met."

"I'm not like a lot of agents," she said. "If Jones asks for my help, I'm willing to give it because I trust him. He had to stay in Chicago on an assignment and he needed someone to stock this house with food and extra clothing. I was glad to do whatever I could to help, despite it going against Director's orders. Sometimes the results outweigh the consequences."

Carrie's eyes were passionate and her kewpie doll mouth was pressed in a serious line. Shane could tell she meant every word she said and was loyal to Jones. That's all he could ask for his friend. "You picked a good one," Shane said to Wildcat. "Though how you got her to fall in love with you is a mystery."

"What can I say? I have charm to spare," Wildcat said with a shrug. "Maybe I can loan you some. You're not looking your best right now."

"I've been shot and lying in bed unconscious for two days. How the hell else am I supposed to look?" Shane turned his attention to Rachel to get her support, but her attention was riveted on the file in front of her.

Shane cursed viciously when he saw the picture of himself in her shaking hands. It was his old FBI photo and the pages attached to it described his job on the Valentine task force. Plain and simple, he'd been the one asked to steady the crosshairs on Rachel's father and pull the trigger if necessary. He thanked God it hadn't been necessary.

"What is this?" Rachel asked.

Wildcat winced and Carrie looked on with sympathy at the both of them. Shane kept his expression blank and wondered how to begin. He might as well get it over with, he thought. She wasn't going to like the outcome either way.

"When I first joined the Hostage and Rescue Unit I was given your father as a target," Shane said, his throat suddenly dry. "In fact he was my very first target. It was a hell of an assignment for someone as new as me to the job."

He remembered the congratulatory slaps on the back and looks of envy from some of his other coworkers. It had made him feel like a king at the time, but now it made him feel like the lowest form of life. His military record had been undisputable, which was why the director had passed the file his way.

Shane got up from the table and went to find the makings for coffee. The silence behind him was deafening as he poured dark grounds into the filter and added water. He tried to find his words carefully, but they stuck in his throat. There could be no more secrets between them if he wanted the chance to have a future with Rachel.

Distracted, Shane left the coffee on the counter and returned to his seat next her. "I wasn't pulled onto the team to assassinate your father. A sniper is not an assassin. That's an important distinction for all of us, and being called to take out a target was never something my unit handled lightly. At the FBI, snipers were called in as a last measure to protect something or someone in imminent danger.

"Intelligence found information that your father had copies of some very important documents from Homeland Security and the military. Documents involving weapons. Intelligence also told us that Dom had set up a meeting with Lex Torrino out in New Jersey to sell the information for several million dollars. It was common knowledge that Lex had ties to terrorist groups, so it was a matter of national security that he never get his hands on those documents. I was set up as a precautionary measure in case the documents were in jeopardy of disappearing. My instructions were to take out both targets if it looked like the briefcase was going to be part of a switch or if Lex got too greedy.

"Dom went to meet Lex in a very public train station at rush hour with the briefcase in hand. They each stopped at a kiosk and grabbed a cup of coffee before finding a table. They were getting down to business when an overzealous agent busted in on them before they could make the transaction. Civilians were everywhere and no one could hear orders over the shouts as agents jumped out of their hiding places with guns drawn. I knew it was a blown mission from that moment, but I had to wait for the FBI to officially cancel my contract to kill. It only took them a couple of minutes to get in touch with me. I didn't even stay around to see what happened. My job was done as far as I was concerned. It turned out Intelligence had been wrong and your father's briefcase had a bunch of real estate papers inside and Dom was going to sell Lex some property he owned in New Jersey."

Even now Shane knew he'd just been doing his job and felt no remorse for what he'd always considered an important service for his country. "It was just a job," Shane said. "One of many I was given over the years. Nothing more. Nothing less."

"If it had come down to it," Rachel asked. "Would you have killed him?"

Shane only hesitated for the barest of seconds before he answered.

"Yes."

Rachel pushed back from the table and walked into her bedroom, shutting the door with a finality that scared the hell out of Shane. Would there ever be a point in his life where the mistakes of his past would stop coming back to haunt him?

Shane went back to the coffee pot and poured himself a large mug of the steaming liquid. Every sip tasted bitter on is tongue. He kept his back turned, wishing for things that could never be when Carrie's soft voice interrupted his private thoughts.

"Let me talk to her," she said. "She'll understand you did what you had to once she has time to think about it."

Shane didn't answer her, but he heard Carrie's light knock and the squeak of hinges a few seconds later.

"Hell, Ace," Wildcat said. "This is my fault. I didn't even think about your information being in the file. I just grabbed it from my home office and drove straight here."

"No, it needed to come out. I should have been honest from the start and told her sooner. She might not hate me so much now if I had."

"You love her," Wildcat said, surprised. "I'll be damned."

Shane took his coffee, tossed Wildcat a bottled water because he knew his friend never touched any kind of caffeine and settled back across from him. "I don't know. I want her, but what I feel for Rachel, it's not like it was with Maggie."

"I'd worry more if it was," Wildcat commented. "They're different people. And you've changed since Maggie died. I'm not saying that what you felt for Maggie should ever be replaced, but that doesn't mean it's all that's left out there for you either. You're still alive, my friend. It's time you started acting like it."

"The last few days have made me realize that more than ever. I think I'm starting to feel my age."

Wildcat leaned back his head and laughed. "Hell, you're only thirty-two. I'm three years older than you, and I'm in the prime of my life. Maybe you need to take some vitamins."

"Yeah, I'm sure that would help," Shane said sarcastically. "Or it could just be the blood loss."

"If you hadn't been sitting behind a desk getting soft for two years, that guy in Tulsa never would have gotten a piece of you."

Shane's only response was a rude hand gesture. "What was the business in Chicago that held you up?" Shane asked. "Does it have to do with Angelo Valentine?"

"You could say that," Jones said. "Christ, this whole thing has been screwed up from the beginning. Angelo's been busy since you and Rachel left New Orleans. Bodies have been washing up from Lake Michigan on an average of one a day."

"Anyone we know?"

"No, but your girlfriend does. Three days ago a tourist noticed Cleopatra Carlisle floating near Navy Pier with the zoom lens of a camera. The body was fairly fresh, and she'd been dead less than a couple of hours. Death was the standard MO used by Angelo himself—throat sliced to the point that the head was barely attached," Jones said, making a slicing motion across his neck with his finger. "The file on Cleo says she was a close friend of Rachel's. They roomed together at Loyola for four years, and Rachel was her maid of honor last Christmas. The husband was away on business at time of death."

"Damn," Shane said, massaging the headache that still pounded behind his eyes. "This is going to be hard on Rachel. She's going to blame herself." He got up and rummaged through one of the drawers until he found the bottle of aspirin. So far it hadn't done anything to relieve the pressure, but he was willing to give it another try.

"Well, it gets worse. The day before yesterday an Agent Jackson Cole washed up about a hundred feet from where the first body was found. Same cause of death as the first victim. He was the new agent in charge of the Valentine case. Word through the office was that Cole had an informer on the inside of Angelo's organization. Apparently Angelo's men aren't too happy with the way things are being run, and there've been a few internal struggles. Director Shaw is mainlining Rolaids and hasn't slept in weeks. His agents keep dying and the higher ups want to know why."

Shane grunted. "Not a good position to be in, for sure. But he's the man in charge, and the leak is in his office, so it's his responsibility. Do you have an idea on the informer in Angelo's organization?"

"Yeah, his name is Sal Lorenzo. He's in the morgue along with Agent Cole, though it took us longer to find all of Lorenzo's body parts. Angelo was sending a message to his other men."

"You said there was another victim who washed up. Who was it?" Shane asked, the feeling in his gut already dreading what Jones was going to tell him.

"Randall Clark III, or Randy as he was known to his friends," Jones said. "He lived across the hall from Rachel for the last several years. According to my sources, they'd dated for a short time and had been briefly engaged their senior year of college before deciding they made better friends than lovers."

Shane's head was reeling. Rachel had been engaged? And now a man she'd been close to and had maybe even loved was dead. How the hell was he going to break the news to her?

"Are you going to tell Rachel?" Jones asked. "Or I could do it if you think she'd take it better from me."

"No, I'll tell her."

"Will she be all right? You've gotten to know her better than anyone over the last few days. Our file on her tells us pitifully little."

"From what I've gathered her father tried to keep her out of his business as much as possible. She's led a pretty quiet life up until now, but she's one of the strongest people I've ever met. She'll be okay. But once the news has sunken in about her friends she's going to be out for Angelo's blood. She's not one to sit back and let others take care of problems for her."

"Don't let her do anything stupid," Jones said. "The FBI still wants that list, and it is widely known now that she has the last remaining copy. I wouldn't be surprised if Angelo wasn't the only mobster looking for Rachel."

"Great. I don't suppose you have any ideas how to get her to the bank in Chicago and back out alive? I've gone through several scenarios, but the outcome never seems very favorable."

"I've had a few thoughts on the subject but nothing is set in concrete. Carrie and I need to head back this afternoon. She's got meetings later today. If you'll agree, let me talk to a couple of people and see if we can get some extra help. It never hurts to have backup. I'll also see if we can find the bank president and keep him in a safe place for a couple of days until we figure out when we want to go in."

"Do whatever you need to do. Just make sure the people you tell won't give Rachel's head to Angelo on a silver platter. Do you have an estimate of when you'll be back?"

"No, but you'll be safe here for the time being. We've taken this house off the books, and Carrie and I are the only ones who know you're here. You have plenty of food and extra clothes. Just stay put until I come back for you." Jones stood and Shane did the same. "Will you take some advice?" he asked.

Shane smiled and thought back to the days when Jones was his commanding officer. "Since when do you ask if you can give advice?"

"Good point, so listen up. Don't wait too long to tell that woman you love her. From the way things are going I think it's something she might need to hear. And it's something you, my friend, need to say. Maybe it'll be just the thing to make the nightmares go away."

"How the hell do you know about the

nightmares?" Shane asked incredulously.

"I work for the FBI. I know everything."

Rachel thought about using the secret exit in the closet and disappearing again. The idea wasn't completely without merit. She could vanish for good this time. Change her hair and get some contacts. She knew who to contact for a passport and new identity, and she had plenty of cash stashed away in a safe place. Maybe she should just leave the country. And keep in touch with no one. Start over completely with a brand new life.

The knock on the door interrupted her plans of escape and she cursed her indecision. The last thing she wanted to do was talk to anyone.

"Rachel," Carrie said as she came into the room. "Do you want to talk about it?"

"No, I don't think that's a good idea. I think this is something best left alone." Rachel lay down on the bed and stretched out her tired muscles. She could fall asleep so easily. All she had to do was close her eyes and drift away, but Carrie had other plans for her. Rachel wasn't in the mood to hear the reasons Shane had chosen the career path he had. And having a woman she barely knew try to explain it made her all the more irritable.

"No one can understand how it feels to be a

sniper unless you are one," Carrie said.

"That's just the truth. I don't know what it's like and Jones doesn't know, even as close as he and Shane are. And you don't know."

"No offense, Carrie, but I'm really not in the mood to hear this right now," Rachel said. She didn't like the combination of pity and understanding she saw in the other woman's eyes. Couldn't she just have some time alone to think without someone coming along and judging her?

"No offense taken," Carrie said. "But I'm going to say what I came to say anyway, and it's up to you whether or not you listen. What Shane did while he was in the military and the FBI was so important. It's a job that's easily overlooked and always underappreciated. The job itself takes a powerful toll on the body and mind, and the stress that comes from it isn't comprehensible to people like you and me. Not everyone can cut it, and the good ones only last so long before they start to burn out. And believe me, I've read Shane's file. He was very, very good."

"Believe it or not, I understand that it was his job and he had no control over his assignments. But I can't reconcile what he was to how I was raised. I love my father very much, and now that my whole family is gone it makes hearing something like that even harder."

"But Shane's not to blame," Carrie said.

"I don't know who's to blame," Rachel said. "Only that someone should be. Shane is just wired differently. I don't understand him. He has great compassion and a need to protect the innocent or those who are weaker, but he doesn't bat an eye at taking lives when given an order. At least with the way things worked in my family, I always knew where everyone stood. Things are more cut and dried than you might imagine in the mob. We celebrated birthdays and weddings and funerals, and when someone was killed their families were taken care of. Does Shane even care that his victims had wives and children?"

"Jones and Shane have been friends a long time," Carrie said. "And from some of the stories I've heard, I can tell you that I think Shane cares too much. He was loyal to his country and to the other men he worked with. Then his wife died and he was left questioning everything he'd stood for his whole life. Everything he'd always believed in. You can't blame a man for his past. We all have things we've done that are better left forgotten. It's the future that counts."

"Yeah, well I don't think we have much of a future," Rachel said.

"You've got to be kidding me," Carrie said with genuine surprise. "That man is completely in love with you. I mean over the moon in love. Open your eyes."

"I think you're wrong. And I understand why he never can be. I've already come to terms with it. He's still hung up on his wife. Still blames himself for her death. How can I compete with a ghost?"

"Just take it from someone who knows how amazing it is to really be in love. Don't give up on the man too soon. Trust me."

Rachel smiled for the first time since they'd been talking. "You and Jones look great together, by the way. Shane's lucky to have friends like you guys. He *needs* friends like you. I have the feeling he's cut himself off from life for too long."

Rachel got up from the bed and gave Carrie a light hug. "I appreciate you following me in here. I guess I did need to talk about it."

"Yeah, well, I was determined not to give you much of a choice," Carrie said with a smile.

"I guess we should go join the guys and see what we missed."

"We're going to have to leave for awhile," Carrie said. "I've got a meeting with my unit later this afternoon that I can't miss, but we'll be back. I'm sure Jones and Shane have thought of something during their male bonding time out there."

There was a knock at the door and Jones stuck his head in. "Are you ready?" he asked.

"Yeah," Carrie said and reached for the hand he held out. The naked devotion in each of their faces was enough to make Rachel's eyes sting.

She and Shane walked them to the door and were left alone together once again. The silence between them lay heavy, and Rachel wasn't sure what she should do next. She twisted her fingers together and finally brought her gaze to Shane's. He stared at her with a mixture of emotions she couldn't interpret. Emotions she didn't want to interpret.

"We need to talk, Rachel," he said.

She nodded her head silently and dreaded whatever was to come.

CHAPTER TWELVE

"What's wrong?" Rachel asked.

"Maybe we should sit down first," Shane said, reaching for her hand so he could lead her to the small couch in the living room.

"I'm not a child," she said, jerking away. "Whatever it is, I can take it."

Shane didn't know where to begin. It seemed like ever since he'd first crossed Rachel's path he'd brought her nothing but heartache and worry.

"Is it my father? Did they find his body?" she finally asked.

Despite her protests he was able to pull her down on the sofa next to him, and she squeezed his hand tightly between hers. The news wouldn't be any easier the longer he waited. It would be best to tell her straight out. "No, it's not your father's body that was found. I'm sorry, Rachel, but it was Cleopatra Carlisle and Randall Clark's bodies that were discovered. It's already been ruled a mob hit by the FBI because of certain calling cards that were left behind at the scene."

Rachel's face paled at the news and her hand went limp in his.

"Cleo's husband? Has he been told?" she asked.

Shane was watching Rachel closely for any signs that she might be close to an emotional breakdown, but other than being cool to the touch, her feelings were buried somewhere deep inside of her. Somewhere he couldn't reach. She was calm, cool and collected. Almost too calm. Something definitely wasn't right with the picture.

"Her husband was away on business at the time of her murder, but he's been notified and is now back in Chicago to see to the arrangements," he said.

"They were married just last year," Rachel said. "The last time I talked to her she was excited because they'd decided to try and start a family right away. They were very much in love. A perfect match."

"I'm so sorry, Rachel. I wish..."

"And what about Randy?" she interrupted. "He

doesn't have any family left living. His parents died when he was twelve, and he was raised by a grandmother. Do you think the FBI would let me make the arrangements for his mass once we get out of hiding? He was Catholic, and he'd want things to be done properly."

"I'm sure something can be arranged," Shane said.

"Good. Well, thank you for telling me. I know it can't have been easy for you," she said and got up from the couch. "I think I'm going to lie down for a little while."

If it hadn't been for the fine tremors in her hands as she rose, Shane would have let her go. But her grief was suddenly so transparent to him he didn't know how he hadn't seen it before. She was holding on by a very thin thread, and she was going to wait until she was alone to break.

"Rachel," he whispered.

"No, Shane, just let me go. I need to be alone." And then her voice broke on a sob and she collapsed into his open arms.

"It's all right, Sugar. Just let it all out." He held her tightly and stroked her hair while her anguish washed over him in waves. He whispered words of love and compassion in her ear, but she was too far gone to understand the significance.

"It's my fault. All my fault," she repeated over and over again.

Her tears soaked his shirt and he knew there was nothing he could do to take away the burden of her guilt. She'd realize soon enough that her uncle would have found a way to hurt her, whether she'd kept in touch with her friends or not.

The tears slowed, though her breath stayed ragged. "They're all gone," she said. "I have no one left. My family and friends, all destroyed because of a choice my father made. One decision that altered the course of so many lives."

He wanted to tell her she wasn't alone and that she never would be, but he knew now wasn't the time or place. "Not all choices are easy, Rachel, and there are consequences that each choice brings. You can't fault your father for wanting to do the right thing."

"No, I can't fault him, but I have to place the blame somewhere. On someone. I can't even think of what's left for me. The hurt just runs too deep. I'm numb with it."

Shane knew only too well how personal pain numbed the soul. There was only one remedy. Time. He held her in his arms for what might have been hours. If he could have taken the pain away he gladly would have, but life didn't work that way.

Her breathing changed and he thought she might have fallen asleep, but her fingers skimmed across the back of his neck and tangled in his hair. A jolt of lust rocketed through his system, and he had to remind himself that it would be all too easy to take advantage of the situation.

"Shane," Rachel whispered.

Her lips brushed against his ear, and he jerked away as if he'd been burned. "No, Rachel. You're not thinking straight, and I don't want to be a substitute for whatever it is you're feeling right now. If we make love. When we make love," he corrected, "it will be because we both want each other more than anything else. There will be no other demons or ghosts getting in the way the next time."

"Please, Shane," she said, kissing her way along his jaw line and the sensitive skin on his neck to his lips. "I need to feel. I need you."

Rachel straddled his hips and his hands spanned her waist, but he wasn't sure if he was trying to push her away or pull her closer. She had the ability, like no one else ever had, to muddle his thinking.

"You'll hate us both in the morning, and that's not something I can live with."

"We'll both live with it," she said. "We'll go into this with no regrets. Don't you understand that I feel dead inside? Make me feel alive again, Shane."

"Not this way." He gathered his resolve and

cursed himself as he pushed her away. He got up from the couch and moved around her in a wide circle, like a lion tamer who was afraid of the lion. The satisfied smile on her lips made it obvious she knew she held all the power, and her eyes were daring him, all but calling him a coward.

She pulled the oversized shirt she wore over her head and tossed it to the floor, exposing the white lace beneath. "You don't play fair, Rachel," he said as the air clogged in his lungs.

"No, I don't. And you, Shane Quincy, have spent too much time being too fair. Too honest. Too noble. I think it's time you took what you wanted and said to hell with everything else."

The snap on her jeans came next, and Shane felt his eyes roll back in his head. The woman definitely knew how to make a statement. She pushed the denim over her hips to reveal a tiny scrap of white lace that should have been illegal.

"I'm trying to do the right thing here, Rachel," he said, backing up as she walked toward him like a lioness stalking her prey. He hit a wall and was consumed by panic. She'd flicked the tiny snap at the front of her bra so her breasts sprang free and all the thoughts in his head vanished. She was beautiful. A vulnerable seductress who would shatter under careless hands. She reached for him but he took her hands in a solid grasp before she could touch him. He didn't want to be careless. Not with her.

“You win, Rachel.” He saw the light of triumph in her eyes masking the hurt. Her breathing was rapid and he could see the pulse pounding in her throat. She was looking for something raw and untamed, and he could feel the beast inside him pressing to escape. “But if we do this,” he said. “We do it my way.”

She looked confused as he grazed a finger over the inside of her wrist. Her pulse jumped and she tried to pull out of his grasp. His touch was tender and her eyes grew wide as his fingers caressed her arms, along her shoulders and collar bone.

“What are you doing?” she asked breathlessly. “I thought you wanted to make love?”

She tried to grab for him and set his pulse racing, but he took hold of her hands again, this time bringing each one to his lips and kissing the tender skin on her palms.

“We are going to make love,” Shane said, looking deeply into her eyes so she knew exactly what he meant.

“No, that’s not what I want.” She pulled against his grasp, but he held tight. “I’m not ready for this.”

“Just relax, Rachel. I’m going to take good care of you.” His breath steadied now that he was back in control, and when his eyes met hers they were calm and confident. His fingers entwined with hers and he lead her to the bedroom—to the bed they’d shared merely hours before. But this time there would be no mindless coupling in the dark. This time things would be different.

Rachel watched as he switched on the bedside lamp and turned down the bed. Simple gestures that shouldn't have made her heart stutter or her palms go damp. But they did. How had things gotten so out of control? It was her own fault. She'd wanted the freedom of release. A few restless minutes that would take her mind off of the misery. But instead she'd gotten more than she'd bargained for. She had a feeling that making love with Shane, making real love, was something that time wouldn't heal. And she wasn't prepared to deal with the aftermath.

"Listen, Shane, I don't think I'm cut out for this...this," she gestured toward the downturned bed and the thick white candles he was lighting. "Romance," she blurted out.

He smiled patiently and came back to her, taking her hands and leading her toward the bed. She wanted to cover her nakedness, but he wouldn't let her. He was still fully clothed, and Rachel had never felt more awkward in her life. She was as nervous as she was the first time, only now it mattered. *This* mattered.

He treated her like porcelain, fragile and precious. Her fingers reached for the edge of his shirt and drew it over his head. His skin was warm and hard against her softness, and she reveled in the different textures of him. His mouth roamed over her lazily, lingering and savoring until she was mad with wanting him.

The scent of his desire overwhelmed her, the rich and heady smell that was a mixture of male and soap. She pressed her face against the hollow of his throat and absorbed him. She was restless beneath him, her body arching against his and her fingers bruising his flesh, but he wouldn't give her what she wanted. He took his time, his mouth soothing against hers as he delved into a kiss hot enough to melt.

Whimpers of delight filled the room and she realized they were coming from her. Had anyone ever paid this much attention to her? Only Shane. His patience was endless and his desire for her maddening. She didn't know there could be so much.

Millions of tiny explosions rocketed through her body as his passions grew with intensity and his needs became greedy. Nothing in her life had prepared her for the depth of feeling she had toward Shane. She'd never made love before. Been loved. And now that she knew what it was like she was afraid she'd never have it again.

But when they finally joined, all the doubts and fears went away. His mouth took hers once again in a scorching kiss, and she clung to him as they plummeted over the edge of oblivion.

CHAPTER THIRTEEN

They spent another two days lost only to each other. They made love and slept and healed, both of them ridding themselves of the wounds they'd learned to live with. They fed their bodies and their souls, telling each other the secrets of their pasts they'd kept concealed for so long. There was no awkwardness between them, only satisfaction and love, though the word had remained unspoken.

It was past midnight and they were both curled together in sleep when they heard the series of beeps telling them someone was about to enter their sanctuary. Shane reached for his gun, unmindful of his nakedness, and he ran into the living room, thinking only of protecting Rachel and giving her a head start to escape.

"Get dressed and get into the other bedroom," he said, his attention on the opening metal door. He saw her out of his peripheral vision and swore. She had the sawed-off shotgun in her hands and was crouched low in the bedroom doorway.

"I'm not leaving you here," she insisted.

"Dammit, Rachel," he said. "Can't you ever..."

"Rise and shine, sleepyheads," a familiar voice interrupted from the entryway. "We've got a plan and a small window of opportunity to take advantage of it," Jones said.

Shane let out a breath and rolled his eyes. "Thanks for the warning, Wildcat. You're lucky you're not standing there with a bunch of holes in you."

"Nah, bullets don't scare me. You should know by now I'm as good as Superman," Jones said, flipping on some lights. "God Almighty, boy. Go put some clothes on. I'm too young to go blind."

"Don't hurry on my account," Carrie called from the doorway, causing Rachel to snicker under her breath.

Shane blushed and hurried past Rachel to get his clothes, mumbling things best left unsaid under his breath.

"Sorry, we weren't expecting anyone this late," Rachel said.

"That's the point," Carrie said, coming in and making herself at home. "Though it wouldn't have hurt Jones to knock first," she said shooting him a dirty look.

"What fun would that be?" Jones countered.

Rachel went into the kitchen and put on a pot of coffee. She knew Shane practically lived on caffeine and poured him a cup just as he came back into the room, fully clothed this time. She stuck with bottled water because her system was already jittery enough now that she knew things were about to come to a head.

"So what's this about a plan?" Shane asked.

"We've got the bank president locked up in a safe place, and I've got men watching Angelo," Jones said. "The bank president didn't really want to help us out, claiming something about normal banking hours and customer privacy, but he was real helpful once I showed him a few photos of what Angelo is capable of. He's a real prissy little fellow. Won't let anyone call him anything but Mr. Norman, and he insisted we let him dress in his normal suit and tie before taking him. All we need now is Rachel and to swing by and pick up Mr. Norman and we can go get the list."

"I hope you've got someone you can trust guarding Mr. Norman," Shane said. "I'd hate to get there only to find he's had his throat slashed."

"I think Cutter and Jax would take offense to that," Jones said.

"Cutter and Jax?" Shane asked, surprised. "You called them in to help with this?" A smile split his face before he could help it. If Wildcat had called in members of the Alpha Squadron to help there was no way they would fail. Shane's adrenaline surged and he found he was looking forward to the night ahead.

"Yeah, you could say they owe me a few favors," Jones said. "The whole team came running as soon as I called. Well, almost the whole team. It took everyone a couple of days to rearrange their schedules and get here, but they were more than glad to help out. Civilian life gets boring after a while. Cutter and Jax are keeping a close eye on Mr. Norman, and Merlin and Dixon are keeping an eye on Angelo's activities. I couldn't get a hold of Doc. He's out of the country on an assignment."

"He'll be pissed he missed the fun," Shane said.

"There's no rest for the wicked." Jones clapped his hands and got down to business. "You guys pack up your stuff and let's get out of here. We're under crunch time."

"Already done," Rachel said, holding up the black bag of guns they'd found. "I haven't breathed fresh air in almost a week, and I'm itching to finally do something instead of just sitting here waiting."

"You might want to put one of the sweatshirts in your drawer on," Carrie said from her relaxed position on the couch. "It's gotten cold over the last few days, and we're supposed to have rain coming soon."

"Thanks, Carrie," Rachel said, noticing for the first time that she and Jones were both wearing jackets over their shoulder holsters. She grabbed a dark sweatshirt from the drawer and another for Shane before rejoining the conversation.

"What do you have in mind once Rachel gets the papers from the vault?" Shane asked. "She's still not safe until they're in the right hands."

"Dominic Valentine's attorney has been in protective custody since Dom went missing with the first set of papers and Agent Culver washed up on shore eight months ago. I'll have Cutter and Jax go pick him up just as soon as we relieve them of their babysitting duties over Mr. Norman. I also have a federal judge lined up to sign search warrants for Angelo's home and businesses."

"What about the other people on the list?" Shane asked. "They're going to be out for blood even when the documents are turned over."

Jones sighed and shrugged his shoulders. "Unfortunately, that's something we have less control over. Until the list Dominic put together has been checked out and confirmed, there's nothing we can do. Rachel will need to go into protective custody until everything is sorted out."

"And how long will that take?" Rachel asked.

"Optimistically, it could be as short as a few weeks. Realistically, it's more likely to be closer to a year," Jones answered.

"No way," Rachel said. "I did just fine for the eight months I was on my own without the FBI's help. There's no way I'm going to be trapped in another place like this one for a whole year. I know how to disappear."

"Yeah, except one of Angelo Valentine's men found you anyway," Shane said.

"I'll admit I made mistakes the last time," she said. "But I promise I can disappear so no one can find me if I really wanted to. And that's exactly what I'll do if they try to force me into being held in protective custody."

"Now, Rachel," Jones said.

"Don't bother," Shane said abruptly. "We'll argue about this later. Let's just get out of here and get things done."

The air was brittle with cold, but Rachel inhaled the icy air with relief. The night was black and the moon barely visible through the gathering clouds in the sky. They left the stolen Honda in the garage and piled into Wildcat's big black SUV.

Rachel knew Shane was angry at her, but it wasn't something that could be helped. She couldn't very well ask him to give up the business he'd created and go on the run with her. That wouldn't be fair at all. And it's not like the future had even come up in the last two days, even though it had seemed that there was some kind of future in store for them.

Rain splattered against the windshield as the navigation system on the dash led them back to civilization. It wasn't until they passed a familiar sight that Rachel knew where they were.

"Why are we back in Joplin? I thought we were going to Chicago?" she asked.

"We've got a private flight chartered to get us there tonight. It's a nine hour drive by car, and I think our sneak attack would lose its effect if we showed up in broad daylight tomorrow," Jones said.

Rachel was obviously too tired to think rationally or she would have realized this already. "How can you keep all of this stuff you're doing for us off the FBI radar?" she asked. "Won't you get in trouble?"

"Nah, but I'm calling in a lot of favors. You're lucky so many people owe me," he said with a cocky smile. For some reason Wildcat's confidence reassured Rachel, and she could tell by looking at Shane that he believed in his friend's abilities with equal certainty.

The Joplin airport looked much different now that they weren't being chased by gun-toting maniacs. Wildcat drove the SUV straight onto the tarmac next to a small twin engine plane that was already running and had the stairs let down for passengers to board. It was obviously a company plane of some sort as the logo on the side read NJEnterprises.

They got out of the SUV and into the steady drizzle. A man stuck his head out of the open door, and Rachel got a glimpse of one of the most handsome men she'd ever seen. He was GQ cover model material, but when she got closer she could see the scar that marred his left cheek and left him not so perfect.

"Let's move it, people," the man said. "The weather's only going to get worse and the temperature's dropping." His head disappeared back into the cabin.

"Son of a bitch," Shane said, pushing her up the short flight of steps after the man. "Is that you, Jax?" he asked when they finally got inside.

"And who the hell else would be flying your ass around? Just like old times, right, Ace?" And then the man smiled and Rachel was caught momentarily speechless. The man was a lethal weapon, and from the wink and slow appraisal he gave her she was willing to bet he knew it.

Shane pulled her close and bared his teeth in a possessive gesture that had her raising an eyebrow. "Rachel, I want you to meet Nikolas Jacks. Don't ever believe anything he ever tells you. Jax, this is Rachel

Valentine, and she's too smart to fall for your Casanova routine. So don't even bother."

"It's a pleasure to meet you, Rachel," Jax said, taking her hand and ignoring the low growl of warning Shane emitted.

He took his time kissing her hand, and the twinkle in his eyes was contagious. She had a hard time not laughing out loud at the easy way he played Shane. She decided he was harmless enough, but probably a handful.

"Are you going to make us stand in the rain all night, Jax, or are we going to ever get this death trap off the ground?" Jones asked from behind.

"Don't get your panties in a twist, Sergeant. Find a seat and get buckled. I'm ready to fly when you are."

"I thought Jax was supposed to be guarding the banker," Shane said to Jones.

"Cutter and I have been babysitting that guy for twenty-four hours," Jax said. "And if Wildcat here hadn't offered me the chance to fly I would have shot the man myself. He's been treating us like we were his damned servants, asking for crushed ice instead of cubed and a relish tray. What in the hell is a relish tray? Believe me when I say Mr. Norman is much safer without me there. Cutter is better at that kind of thing anyway."

"What kind of thing?" Shane asked. "Being around other people without wanting to kill them?"

"Basically," Jax said with a shrug. "The human race is just no damned good."

"I've told you more than once I know the name of a good therapist who would probably help you get over this phobia you have," Jones said. "Now, both of you get the hell out of my way so I can sit down. Some of us work for a living and are tired."

There were a few good natured shoves between the men as they made their way into the small cabin. There was only enough seating for the four of them, but the chairs were oversized and made of light grey supple leather. Rachel sat in the window seat and Shane sat down next to her, immediately reclining his seat back and closing his eyes. The rain outside was hypnotic as it misted over the bright lights on the runway, but Rachel couldn't relax.

"We're cleared for takeoff," Jax said from over speaker. "We'll arrive at Midway in about an hour and a half. I'm sorry to say this is probably going to be a bumpy ride with the weather the way it is. Stay buckled and grab some shut eye while you can."

That was easy for him to say, Rachel thought. The last thing she could think of right now was sleep. There were too many doubts, too many worries, playing havoc in her brain. She looked over at Carrie and Jones and saw they were already preserving their energy with a nap. And Shane was no better beside her. Wasn't anyone worried besides her? If the plan didn't work, they could all be dead by morning.

Shane reached over and took her hand and squeezed it gently, telling her without words to relax. His touch did amazing things to her body, and she almost believed everything was going to turn out all right when he was near.

The plane taxied down the runway, and the rain pelted against the windows harder. The plane shook and shuddered as it lifted into the air, defying gravity and taking on the storm around them. The plane dipped and she felt her stomach rise just before it gained altitude again. She squeezed Shane's hand tighter and tried to think positive thoughts. Like maybe crashing and burning in a plane the size of a tin can was much more preferable over being tortured to death by her Uncle Angelo.

Then again, maybe not.

The plane shuddered once more and the engines went silent just before the lights went off inside the cabin.

CHAPTER FOURTEEN

Rachel still had her arms around Jax after Shane had stowed all of their bags in another black SUV that was waiting for them at Midway International Airport, and from the look on Jax's face he wasn't minding the attention one bit. Jones and Carrie were already in the front seats of the SUV and the engine was running. It was just past two in the morning and their window of opportunity was shrinking with every minute.

"Unhand my woman," Shane said, rolling his eyes and jerking Rachel away from Jax's embrace. "You'd think the man did something special by the way you keep fawning over him," he said to Rachel. "He doesn't need any help expanding his ego."

"Don't be jealous, Shane. There was a moment back there when you were looking pretty worried," Rachel said. "Just because Jax managed to work miracles and bring that sardine can on wheels back to earth safely doesn't mean you should be rude."

Shane laughed at Jax's indignant expression once he heard Rachel call his pride and joy a sardine can on wheels. "Let's go, Sugar," he said, giving Jax a smug smile over his shoulder.

"But what about Jax? Shouldn't he be coming with us?"

"Should I be worried about this odd fascination you have with Jax?" Shane asked, shaking his head.

"Well, he did just save my life. Yours too. But I think it's cute when you're jealous."

Shane rolled his eyes. "Yeah, right. Jax has got a few things to see to with the plane, but he'll follow behind and grab Cutter so they can pick up your father's attorney from protective custody."

They headed east out of Midway and into the residential area of Chicago. The lights from the city could be seen in the distance, but these neighborhoods they were driving through were all hidden in shadow. What few streetlights there were had been broken out, and shards of glass littered the streets along with trash and the occasional homeless person. All of the houses were attached to each other and were no wider than one room across. The sidewalks were cracked and the trees were empty of leaves. Nothing could hide the stark depression of the street or the desperation behind the crumbling brick of the houses.

They stopped in front of the last house on the block, and Jones pulled into a cracked driveway that had weeds growing between the broken concrete. The rain had lessened back to a miserable drizzle, and the headlights from the SUV caught a glimpse of the whites of someone's eyes as they lighted the alleyway. Carrie already had her gun in her lap, and Shane grabbed the .9mm out of the small of his back.

"Nice neighborhood," Rachel commented.

"We figured it was the least we could for Mr. Norman since he was so accommodating," Jones said. "You kids stay in the car, and Carrie and I will relieve Cutter of Mr. Norman. My best advice is to just shoot anything that moves or they'll have this car stripped before we make it back outside."

Jones and Carrie left the SUV with their weapons drawn and in plain sight of anyone lurking in the area. The silence was deafening inside the car, and Rachel was sure she saw movement just outside her window, though she couldn't be sure. There were a few people who dashed back and forth from the alley to the other houses on the block, but Rachel could never get a clear glimpse of them. They were like rats scurrying from place to place, scavenging whatever they could find.

It was less than five minutes before Rachel saw the outline of Jones backlit at the front door of the row house. He held a small man by the arm and Jones yanked him down the steps and into the rain. By the way the man was struggling, it didn't look like he was too happy to see Jones again. Carrie followed closely behind them with her weapon out and her eyes constantly moving as she looked for danger.

The back door of the SUV opened next to Rachel and the small man was unceremoniously tossed in next to her like a sack of potatoes. The man reminded her of a small wet cat. Rachel scooted closer to Shane and felt much better when he put his arm around her. Jones and Carrie got back in the front seat, and they were back on the road in no time.

"I tell you, I'm going to be filing a complaint with your superior, young man," the nasally voice from beside her said.

Rachel saw Wildcat's hands tighten on the steering wheel, but he kept his eyes on the road ahead. He turned onto the highway and almost immediately the neighborhoods improved. They were now headed into the heart of the city.

"I've never been treated so poorly in my entire life," the man said, turning his gaze on Rachel. He was small of stature and his sandy hair was thinning on top. Thick glassed perched at the end of his nose and his fingernails were buffed and manicured. Despite his damp and wilted appearance, the quality of his suit was very expensive, as was the gold watch at his wrist.

"I was snatched from my home in the middle of the night, and they wouldn't even give me the courtesy of packing a bag first. For two days I've had to wear these clothes. It's just shameful. And then, as if that weren't bad enough, they blindfolded me and took me to this God forsaken place. I haven't slept a wink in fear the rats would eat me alive. And then those barbarians showed up and watched every move I made. I couldn't even use the facilities in private. It's just been a dreadful experience."

Rachel nodded sympathetically and let him wind down. The man was close to hyperventilation and was obviously prone to hysterics. She scooted closer to Shane, though she was practically sitting on his lap as it was.

"Oh dear, I haven't introduced myself. This situation has just taken its toll on my nerves. I'll have to have two sessions next week with my therapist. I'm Neville Norman, by the way," he said, extending his hand. "Third generation president and owner of Suretrust Bank."

He didn't give Rachel the opportunity to introduce herself. "And you must be Rachel Valentine. I've seen your picture on the news, so that's how I recognized you. Though you're not quite what I expected now that I'm seeing you in person for the first time. I thought you'd have a little more...class," he said, looking at her sweatshirt and jeans with disapproval. "Did you know you're wanted by the police for murder?"

Rachel was speechless. Was this guy for real?

"But of course you know," he said, shaking his head. "You're with the police right now. And it seems you have your father's talent for buying your way out of sticky situations since you're not being hauled away in handcuffs."

Rachel narrowed her eyes and felt Shane put a restraining hand on her shoulder. Mr. Norman must have seen her disgusted look because he backpedalled fast.

"Don't get me wrong, my dear. I'm so pleased you chose my bank for your nefarious purposes. According to my bank manager, people are opening new accounts left and right because of the notoriety. I'm afraid someone on my staff might have told the media you're a customer, and I do give my apologies for that, my dear, and promise to reprimand the guilty party right away. But business has really picked up. And with the economy the way it is too," he said, shaking his head.

"Glad I could be of help," Rachel said stiffly.

"And now it's my turn to help you," Mr. Norman said. "And maybe you'll think about transferring all of your father's assets over to Suretrust once he's declared legally dead."

Before Rachel could say anything to the disgusting little man, Carrie turned around in her seat and leveled her gun right between his eyes. “Mr. Norman,” she said sweetly. “Kindly shut up.”

Carrie waited until she saw his nod of agreement before turning back around in her seat. Rachel saw the grin on Wildcat’s face and had to duck her head down so her own smile couldn’t be seen. Shane was looking out the window of the SUV, but she could feel his body shaking with laughter.

The rest of the trip was made in silence.

Suretrust Bank was directly across the street from Loyola University. It was one of the reasons Rachel had originally chosen it. When she’d first opened her account she’d been a student at the university and it had seemed the most convenient place to do her business.

Contrary to what others thought, she hadn’t lived on the money her father continuously deposited into her account. She’d had a job all the way through college to supplement the athletic scholarship she’d received for target shooting, and she’d made meager deposits every week for four years. If only she’d known about Neville Norman’s tendencies for high drama and his big mouth back then, she would have gladly made the trek across the city to a different bank every week.

Mr. Norman was given permission to speak again once the bank came into view. He led them around the back of the building to the employee entrance, and Jones parked the SUV so it blocked the back entrance.

The bank was housed in what used to be an old Catholic Church built some time in the mid-1850's. The architecture was gothic, similar to most of the churches built during that time in Chicago, and they hadn't changed the outside much when it had been converted into a bank during the early part of the twentieth century. They'd replaced the stained glass on the street level with sturdier material and had them wired with alarms, but the stained glass on the upper floors where all the offices were held was as it always had been.

"I hope you all understand how inconvenient this is for me and my bank," Mr. Norman said. "We would have gotten national news coverage if you'd brought Ms. Valentine in to collect her things during peak traffic hours."

"We're sorry for the inconvenience," Jones said as diplomatically as possible. "But perhaps it would be best if you opened the doors and let us in before any of Angelo Valentine's men decide to use us for target practice."

Mr. Norman paled at that bit of news and hurried to the back door. Carrie and Shane kept Rachel between them, and she didn't like the fact that they were risking their own lives trying to protect hers.

Mr. Norman opened the outer door with a key and moved into a short entryway that was barred with an electronic gate. He punched in a long series of numbers on a keypad and held his thumb to a scanner. The bars around them lifted from the ground and into the ceiling.

"No lights," Jones ordered as Mr. Norman was about to hit the main switch. "We draw as little attention as possible to ourselves."

An urgency she couldn't explain started to hammer away at Rachel's insides, and she looked behind her nervously, afraid Angelo's men were hiding around the corner. Something didn't feel right, and from the way the others held onto their weapons and swept slowly throughout the building, she thought they might be having the same feelings.

"Rachel, which direction is your safety deposit box?" Shane asked.

"I can answer that," Mr. Norman said as if he were the star pupil in a classroom. Using his keys to unlock a drawer behind the main counter, he pulled out a large key ring that held dozens of numbered silver keys. "Ms. Valentine purchased the VIP safety deposit box, which is housed in the basement level of the building. And as with all our VIP customers, only the best security will do," he said proudly.

Rachel rolled her eyes, perfectly aware of what

kind of safety deposit box she had and where it was located in the building, but she let Mr. Norman prattle on because despite his irritating personality, she could sense the layer of tension he was hiding behind the professional façade.

"We'll have to take the stairs down," Mr. Norman said apologetically. "We felt adding elevators would be compromising the integrity of the structure."

The stair railings were dark and polished to a high gleam, and the stairs themselves were grey-veined white marble. Rachel followed behind Mr. Norman down the stairs to the basement level. There were ornate sconces lining each side of the walls on the way down, and they cast only a small yellow glow in the darkness.

"I'm assuming I can turn the lights on down here," Mr. Norman said insolently to Jones.

"By all means," Jones said.

Mr. Norman flipped on several switches beside a round steel door and harsh fluorescent lighting came on overhead. He typed in yet another key code for the door and used his keys before turning the handle. The room wasn't terribly large. Rachel guessed an independent bank only had a handful of what they considered VIP customers. The walls were lined with numbered silver boxes and there were heavy stainless steel tables in rows down the middle of the room. The sterility of the room didn't match the rest of the bank at all.

“Now, Ms. Valentine,” Mr. Norman said. “All you need to do is use your key and collect your belongings. I can have everyone wait outside and give you some privacy if it makes you more comfortable.”

“But I don’t have my key,” Rachel said. “It was in my apartment when it caught fire. I didn’t have time to get it.”

Mr. Norman clucked his tongue and shook his head. “Then I’m afraid I’ll need two valid forms of ID before I can open it for you. We’ll need to go back upstairs and fill out the proper paperwork. You do have ID, don’t you?”

“Not on me,” Rachel said with a hesitant smile.

“Open the door, Mr. Norman,” Shane said.

“But it’s against bank policy. If I do it for you and the word gets out, others will expect me to do the same. Or worse, they’ll worry about the safety of their deposits and go elsewhere. I’m sorry, but it just can’t be done. She’ll have to come back when she has proper identification or the key. It’s the best I can do.”

Shane moved as fast as lightning, grabbing Mr. Norman by the shirt collar and holding him off the ground. Mr. Norman’s face was turning purple, but Shane showed no signs of distress. “Open her box now, Mr. Norman, or I’m going to throw you through that wall over there. Nod if you understand me."

Mr. Norman nodded and Shane dropped him to the floor in a heap. He scrambled off the ground and looked through the numbered keys with shaking hands. Rachel took the wad of keys from him and walked to the far corner of the room where her box was located. Mr. Norman managed to get up off the ground with minimal fuss. He flitted around nervously, wringing his hands, either concerned the bank propriety police were going to come through the door and arrest him or Shane was going to break every bone in his body. From the way he was eyeing Shane, she had a feeling it was the latter.

"I want to press charges against this…this brute," Mr. Norman said to Jones. "You were a witness to the way he treated me. You're an FBI agent, sworn to uphold the law."

"I don't know what you're talking about," Jones said. "I didn't see anything of the kind."

"We don't have time for this," Shane said, turning his back on Mr. Norman, but Mr. Norman grabbed his sleeve and wouldn't let him leave.

"Arrest him," Mr. Norman said, voice shrill. "I demand it." The three men were gathered in the corner, Shane's face growing dark with rage and Jones trying to contain his laughter as Mr. Norman listed each of Shane's transgressions.

Rachel ignored the argument going on behind

her and focused on the lock box. It took her two tries to get the key into the lock. The nervous tension had only increased the longer they were in the bank. There were too many possibilities. Too many things that could go wrong once she had the papers in her hands. When the lock snicked open, relief consumed her. It was almost the end now. She feared her life would never be "normal" again, but if the FBI did their jobs and shut down the dangerous players on the list, maybe she could begin to live day-to-day without looking over her shoulder. Rachel pulled the rectangular silver box out of the wall and placed it on one of the heavy tables.

"Do you have it?" Carrie asked from the doorway.

The envelope with her name and address on it was exactly where she'd left it eight months before. Rachel grabbed it and shoved the box back into the wall. She just wanted to get out, and get out fast.

Rachel went to stand by Carrie in hopes the men would quit arguing and notice she'd done what she came to do.

"We need to get out of here," she said to Carrie. "I'm not having good feelings about being here. Do you think you can get their attention?"

"I think that can be arranged," Carrie said.

Before Rachel could blink, Carrie had an arm wrapped around her throat, cutting off her air. The discharge of Carrie's gun was deafening in the small room, and Rachel watched in horror as Mr. Norman fell to the floor. Blood pooled beneath his head and ran so dark it was almost black.

"Carrie," Jones said, his weapon out automatically at the sound of gunfire. "What have you done?" The devastation and realization on his face was almost unbearable to look at.

"Don't pretend like I didn't just do you a favor," she said. Carrie positioned Rachel in front of her so the men didn't have a clear shot of her body. "I've wanted to shoot him since the first time I met him."

"I don't understand," Jones said, trying to make sense of the betrayal. "Your career. Everything you've worked for. They'll send you to prison. What about us?"

Rachel's heart went out to Jones. He was confused and hurt, but his training wouldn't let him lower his weapon. Rachel wondered if it came down to it if Jones would be able to pull the trigger.

"Well, here's the thing Jones," Carrie said. "There never really was an us."

A second shot sounded near Rachel's ear and she saw the bloom of red on the front of Wildcat's shirt and the look of surprise on his face as he dropped to his knees. His weapon skidded away from his body, and he touched the wound in his chest before falling over. Rachel's ears rung and she thought she screamed out, but she couldn't be sure.

"Men are so sensitive when they're the ones who are being dumped," Carrie said in her ear. "It's pathetic."

Rachel struggled against the vise of Carrie's arms but her grip was too strong, and Rachel whimpered when Carrie pulled hard on her hair to get her to cooperate.

Mr. Norman's eyes were open and staring and she could only see the smallest movements of Wildcat's chest as he struggled to breathe. Rachel prayed the same fate didn't befall Shane. She kept her eyes locked on Shane's face, mentally telling him how much she loved him, but Shane was focused on Carrie. Shane's gaze didn't waver even as his friend lay bleeding at his feet. His .9mm was pointed at Carrie and his hand was steady.

"Carrie, this isn't the way," Shane said. "I won't hesitate to pull the trigger like Jones. I shoot to kill. Let Rachel go."

"You know I'm not going to do that, lover boy," Carrie said. "I'm making a lot of money on this deal, and I always deliver exactly what the client wants."

Her voice was different, Rachel thought. Rougher and less refined than the woman she'd thought she'd known. Hell, they'd never really known her at all. Only a few days. But Wildcat had been fooled for much longer. It took a true psychopath to live a double life of treachery and feel no remorse for the people you destroyed along the way.

"You killed the other FBI agents working the Valentine case," Shane said.

Carrie shrugged and tightened her grip around Rachel's throat. "Just Agent Culver," she said. "Angelo hired me to bring him Dom, and Culver was in the way. Culver was a casualty of war, but I can't claim responsibility for the other agents. I was just the inside source for information. Angelo's men took care of the rest."

"You know Angelo isn't going to let you live once you've done what he hired you to do. That's the way Angelo works. You're smart enough to know that, Carrie."

"Angelo Valentine is a fool and his men know it," she said. "It wasn't hard to buy a few of them for extra insurance. Now I've got Rachel and the list, and as soon as I hand her over and the money is transferred my job is done. I've been Angelo's inside source for more than two years. Do you think I'm completely stupid? I've got a few tricks up my sleeve that Angelo will never see coming." Carrie backed out of the room so she and Rachel stood at the base of the stairs.

"I'm not letting you leave here with Rachel, Carrie," Shane said. He started to move forward slowly so he could keep them both in sight.

“Stop right there,” Carrie yelled, her voice breaking. The pressure was starting to get to her and her grip became so smothering that Rachel saw spots in front of her eyes. Carrie moved the gun so it was pointed at Rachel.

“You don’t have a choice in the matter,” Carrie said, calmer now. “Put your gun down before I shoot your girlfriend in the thigh. You can hope she doesn’t bleed to death before I hand her over to Angelo. It doesn’t matter one way or the other to me at this point.”

Shane had lived his life by playing the odds, and he knew if he lowered his weapon then she’d put a bullet into his heart. And he’d be no good to Rachel dead. He kept his gun pointed at Carrie’s head and hoped for a clear shot, but luck wasn’t on his side. “That’s not going to happen,” he said, hoping he’d made the right choice.

“You like to live dangerously,” Carrie said. “I guess she doesn’t mean as much to you as I’d thought.”

Shane didn’t look at Rachel, afraid of what he might see in her expression. He was playing a game with a madwoman, and any distraction or break in his focus would get them all killed. Shane prayed Rachel could forgive him when it was all over.

“You lose Shane,” Carrie taunted. “I know every trick in the book, and you can’t bluff your way out of this one." Carrie backed them up the stairs, and Rachel tried to slow her down as much as possible by becoming dead weight in her arms. "Enough!" Carrie said, pressing the gun hard enough to Rachel's thigh to leave a bruise. "I'll do it. I swear. If I hit an artery you'll be dead in a matter of minutes."

"Do as she says, Rachel," Shane called out. Rachel immediately stopped her struggles and went with Carrie higher up the stairs.

"Say goodbye to your lover," Carrie whispered in her ear.

"No!" Rachel screamed, fear gripping her like it never had before at the thought Shane's life could be over in a matter of moments. She forgot about the threat of being shot and struggled frantically to try and dislodge Carrie's grip on her. Carrie took her gun and slammed it across the side of Rachel's face. Her cheek throbbed in pain and the taste of blood filled her mouth so rapidly she was choking on it. She was momentarily stunned by the blow and went limp in Carrie's arms.

"It was nice knowing you," Carrie said to Shane as she pulled something small and round out of her jacket pocket and threw it into the open door of the safety deposit box room.

Rachel didn't even have the strength to scream as Carrie pushed her the rest of the way up the stairs and all hell broke loose behind her.

Shane saw the tiny black object that Carrie threw into the room and only had a moment to react. He kicked the metal table in front of him to its side and ducked behind it, throwing his body over Wildcat's to protect both of them as much as possible. There was nothing he could do to save Mr. Norman, but there was still life left in Wildcat, no matter how little it was.

The explosion rocketed through the entire room and pieces of metal and concrete flew from every direction. His ears rang from the force of the blast and his body shook from the vibrations. Shane shielded the back of his neck with his hands and hunkered over Wildcat, protecting his friend as best he could while the metal table they were hiding behind buckled and folded around them.

The heat was unimaginable, as the metal and concrete in the room made it feel as if they were trapped in an oven. Shane's mind was racing and he knew he had to stay in control to find Rachel alive. But the first order of business was making sure he stayed alive.

The smoke was thick in the room and it was almost impossible to see, but the debris finally stopped falling. Shane pushed at the heavy pieces of metal and concrete that covered his back and felt the sting of the raw scrapes over his body. The wound in his shoulder had reopened and his arm was slicked with blood, but time was of the essence and the adrenaline coursing through his body masked the pain.

He needed to get Jones out and get him help. It was obvious Jones' lung had been pierced by the bubbling pink foam around the wound.

"Come on, buddy, don't give up on me now," Shane said. The muscle Jones had added over the past couple of years added extra weight to his body, and Shane struggled to lift him into his arms. He picked his way over the debris carefully, trying not to jar his friend too much. By the time Shane reached the top of the stairs, sweat dampened his brow and the scrapes on his back and the wound in his shoulder were screaming with pain.

The cold night air and rain felt like heaven against Shane's tortured body when he finally made it out the back door of the bank. He laid Jones gently on the pavement and wondered how long it would be until emergency vehicles began to arrive. His friend was fading fast, the wheeze coming from his chest more prominent and the blue tinge around his lips growing darker in hue.

Shane was relieved to see that the SUV they'd arrived in was still in the parking lot, which meant that Carrie'd had someone waiting for her with another source of transportation. Probably one of Angelo's men. He opened the door of the SUV and rummaged around inside until he found what he was looking for. A Snickers bar sat in the glove compartment. Shane carefully removed the thin plastic wrapping and opened it so it was completely flat. He tossed away the chocolate and grabbed the wrapper and the phone Jones had plugged into the cigarette lighter.

He ran back to his friend and stripped off the sweatshirt he was wearing, placing it under Wildcat's head. Wildcat's eyes were open and dilated and his breathing was shallow and raspy. Shane tore his friend's shirt down the middle and exposed the tiny wound in his chest. He placed the candy wrapper over the hole and held it in place. The wheeze of air stopped leaking from Wildcat's lung and his breathing eased.

"Dammit, I don't have anything to hold this in place," Shane said. His hands were slicked with blood and he looked around for anything that he could tie around Wildcat's chest to keep the candy wrapper in place and pressure on the wound.

"In the back of the truck," Wildcat gasped out.

"Don't talk," Shane ordered. He placed Wildcat's hand against the wound and noticed the thready pulse in his wrist. "Leave your hand here, and press as hard as you can. I'll be right back."

Shane went to the back of the SUV and rummaged around until he found a black windbreaker that would fit around Wildcat's chest. Or at least he hoped it would. Shane ran back to his friend and propped him up so Wildcat was resting against

Shane's knees.

"Here we go," Shane said, tying the sleeves of the jacket tightly over the wound. It would by them a little time, but not much if emergency help didn't arrive soon. "Help is on the way," he assure Jones. "Just hold on."

Shane scrolled through the numbers on the phone he'd found in the SUV until he located the one he was looking for. He waited impatiently for someone to pick up on the other line, and when the voice answered he didn't waste time on small talk.

"This is Jax."

"Wildcat's been shot, and it's critical," Shane said. "He's got a punctured lung. Carrie is Angelo's insider, and she's taking Rachel to Angelo as we speak. Get in touch with Merlin and Dixon and make sure they don't lose sight of Angelo. He'll want to finish things tonight and clean up any loose ends." Shane heard the sirens in the distance and noticed Jones was struggling to stay conscious. "Call me back at this number with a rendezvous point so we can all meet."

Shane hung up the phone and felt the pulse at Wildcat's neck. His heart was working overtime, pumping blood faster and faster even as his pulse grew weaker. Wildcat's eyes were dilated, and Shane thought he was probably going into shock.

"Dammit, Wildcat, you're not a quitter. I thought

bullets couldn't touch you."

The ghost of a smile played around his friend's mouth. The sirens drew closer. "Get out of here," Jones said weakly. Blood tinged his lips as he talked and Shane fought to keep down the surge of panic.

"I'm not leaving you," Shane said. "We all leave together. That's the rule."

"I'm your commanding officer," Jones said, coughing. "Get out of here so you can save her. They'll be here soon to take care of me, but they'll arrest you if you stay. There's nothing more you can do. I've been closer to death than this before. I'll be okay."

Shane clenched his hands into fists and wished for something to punch, something hard that would hurt and take some of the pain he was feeling away. It went against every amount of training he'd ever had to leave Wildcat wounded and possibly dying in the rain.

"That's an order, Marine," Wildcat said with a last burst of strength.

Shane got up from the ground and pivoted sharply on the ball of his foot. His ears were buzzing and tears stung his eyes. He got into the SUV and pulled out of the parking lot, never looking back.

Shane drove around the outskirts of Chicago for no more than half an hour before the cell phone jingled in his pocket and Jax told him the rendezvous point was the same place they'd picked up Mr. Norman. Merlin and Dixon were waiting with information, so he turned the SUV south. Shane wasn't looking forward to going back to the neighborhood, but they didn't have a lot of options since it was best if none of them were seen involving themselves in FBI business, especially since Wildcat was no longer in the picture. Shane wasn't sure what his buddies had been up to the last couple of years, but if they'd all turned civilian like he had then they were putting themselves in a lot of risk.

Shane didn't bother with the driveway once he found his way back to the dilapidated row house. He pulled the SUV across the lawn and parked right in front of the door. A Hummer and a pickup truck were already occupying space in the driveway, and he hoped one of the vehicles would still be intact when they were ready to leave.

The front door of the house opened before he was out of the truck, and Jax stood in the doorway. No words were spoken as Shane made his way into the house. Lives were at stake and there was no time for the celebration they'd normally share at getting to work together on a job once again.

Everyone was gathered in the kitchen area, if it could even be called that, and they were already dressed for the party in black fatigues. Dixon's tall, lanky body sat erect in a straight-backed chair and he worked a toothpick nervously back and forth between his teeth. His dark blond hair was combed back from his face and tortoise shell glasses covered his somber gray eyes. A thin black laptop sat open on the table in front of him.

Merlin sat in the chair opposite Dixon with a roll of what looked like blueprints in his hands. He was Dixon's complete antithesis—dark and stocky in build, skimming just under six feet, and his black hair was unruly and rumpled like he'd just gotten out of bed. A thin scar slashed just above his right eyebrow, giving him a dangerous look that he more than deserved.

Cutter stood with his back to the wall and his arms crossed over his chest. He was almost as broad across the shoulders as Wildcat, but he didn't have the height. His hair was the color of burnished mahogany and he'd grown a short beard since the last time Shane had seen him. His coloring betrayed his Irish roots, and direct green eyes took in everything at once.

Jax stood at his back while Shane took the last available chair. Jax was the cleanup guy—the man you always wanted at your back if you wanted to come out of a situation alive. He'd gotten the scar that ran from the top of his ear to the base of his cheek and ruining the pretty boy persona he'd lived with his entire life by watching their backs in a night raid in Iraq. They would all be dead if Jax hadn't made the sacrifice.

"Were you able to pinpoint a location for where Angelo has Rachel hidden?" Shane asked.

Merlin unrolled the blueprints onto the table. "Angelo and several of his men left his house just minutes after Jax called us and told us what had happened. They took two separate cars from the Valentine estate down Michigan Avenue to a high-rise office building that is currently under construction. Our boy Dixon did a little digging and found that the building is owned by VCorp, which is one of the companies Valentine owns to make things seem more legitimate when it comes to tax time."

"Did you see Rachel in the building?" Shane asked.

"Negative," Merlin said. "There are more than twenty floors in the building. We can only assume that's where he's keeping her as he's got men posted at all the exits, and he didn't look like he was in any hurry to leave the building."

Shane looked at the blueprints and wondered how they were ever going to find her before it was too late. It was worse than searching for a needle in a haystack. "Are any of the floors occupied?" he asked. "And can we get a visual inside from anywhere in the area?" Shane directed the question at Dixon since he was the one who could use his computer skills to break into any database in the world. The talent had come in handy more than once, and Shane was counting on it to help them this time.

Dixon's slow southern drawl often misled people about his intelligence, which according to Dixon, always gave him the upper hand. "Well, tax records show that several businesses occupy the spaces between floors twelve and eighteen." Dixon opened his computer and hit a few buttons so a screen of names and numbers showed up. "But a closer look at these companies show they don't really exist at all. I hacked into a few of the past surveillance tapes and there's never anyone shown going in or out of the building. It's just a dummy operation as far as I can see."

He hit another series of commands and the blueprints came up on screen. "I've blacked out the floors where the offices are located. My gut says he wouldn't use those to hold anyone hostage. It would be inconvenient if the IRS showed up on his doorstep and wanted to take a look around."

Shane could read between the lines. What Dixon really meant was that Angelo wouldn't want to take the chance of dirtying the furnished areas with anything like blood. Shane put the thought out of his mind that even as he was sitting here trying to find a way to save Rachel, she could already be past the point of saving.

"Floors one through twelve are in the skeleton phase of renovations," Dixon continued. "But I'd bet my money that he's got her stashed either on nineteen or twenty. Renovations are a little further along on the upper floors. From what I can tell he's turning them into apartments of sorts."

"Can we get access?" Shane asked.

"Well, that's going to be a little trickier seeing as how there's just the five of us against at least twelve men that we saw guarding the building. Maybe more. The Hancock Hotel is directly across the street from the building, and it should give you a good view of those top two floors from the roof level. You can set up over there and the rest of us will go in on foot and take out as many as we can to give you plenty of time and the best shot possible."

Shane broke out in a cold sweat at the thought of what he was going to have to do. Hadn't he been in almost the exact same situation two years ago? And failed miserably? Now the woman he loved, because there was no doubt now what he felt for Rachel, was putting all her trust and her life in his hands. God, he hoped the saying was wrong about history repeating itself.

"Are you okay, Ace?" Cutter asked.

"Yeah," Shane said, standing. "Let's get a move on. We've only got a couple of hours until daylight."

CHAPTER FIFTEEN

Icy cold water hit Rachel in the face and brought her gasping to consciousness. She didn't remember the drive to wherever she was now or how long she'd been unconscious. She only remembered the fiery explosion in the basement of the bank and that Shane was buried somewhere in the rubble.

She'd screamed and fought against Carrie, not caring about her own safety, and she'd tried to run back down the stairs and into chaos. She remembered Carrie's arms struggling to hold her and that someone else had been there. That's when the second blow had come and it had felt like the back of her skull had exploded. It was lights out after that.

Her vision was blurred and the icy water wracked her body with chills. Her thoughts were scattered and her mind wouldn't cooperate as she tried to piece things together. The right side of her face ached with every laborious breath she took and her eye was swollen almost completely shut. The fierce headache throbbing through her skull was from the blow to the back of the head she'd received. She tried to take stock of the rest of her body, but she couldn't assess the damage since her ankles were tied to a chair with sturdy rope and her hands were cuffed behind her.

"Rise and shine, sleeping beauty," Carrie's voice sang out. "We wouldn't want your uncle to make the trip all this way only to find you'd passed out. It's more fun to torture when the victim is awake. I'm sure you understand that."

Rachel's wet hair hung down in front of her face and she didn't have the strength to raise her head and give Carrie the glare she deserved. Her vision swam and she had to focus to stay conscious.

"I hope he kills you," Rachel rasped. Her throat was dry and the words protested as she tried to force them out. "I'll be glad to watch you die, but I promise you if he doesn't that I will hunt you down and do it myself."

"Ooh, that's scary," Carrie said. Her casual laugh chilled Rachel's blood. "Are you going to come back as a ghost and haunt me?"

Rachel gritted her teeth and forced her head up so she could look Carrie in the eyes, ignoring the pain that was radiating from her skull. Carrie was still dressed in FBI black and her weapon was holstered at her side. But it was her face that gave Rachel the chills. How could anyone be that good of an actress when the insanity was so transparent behind the eyes? Blood was smeared on her cheek and her blond hair was matted and mussed from the aftershocks of the explosion.

"You won't get away with what you did to Shane. To Jones. You're a sick woman. Beyond anyone's help. Which means hell is too good for you. So I'll do whatever I have to do," Rachel swore. "As long as it means you're dead."

Carrie's smile froze in place at the look Rachel gave her. Both women were determined not to back down, but there was fear inside Carrie that hadn't been there a moment ago. An elevator pinged in the distance and footsteps echoed on the concrete floors. Rachel took a moment to look at her surroundings and try to figure out where she was.

She was surrounded by windows. And from the view she knew she was fairly high up. The lights from the hotels and other businesses shone through the windows and lit the floor she was occupying. Stacks of lumber and buckets of paint were scattered around the room, and the metal folding chair she was sitting in seemed to be the only furniture.

The sight of her Uncle Angelo walking into the room was her worst nightmare come true. He looked so much like her father it brought a pang to her heart, but looks was where the similarities ended. Angelo had a cruelty to him that her father had never possessed. Even with the position of power over the mob Dom had obtained over the years, he'd never resorted to cruelty to get what he wanted. And for a time the other mob families had respected that and followed the same guidelines he'd set.

Angelo clucked his tongue at the sight of her. "Well, niece, I've certainly seen you looking better. The swelling on your face might make it harder for the authorities to identify your body. But don't worry. I'm sure they'll figure it out sooner or later. The FBI has ways of finding such things out. Isn't that right Agent Layne?" he asked Carrie.

Rachel could only handle one threat at a time so didn't bother looking at her Uncle Angelo. She'd yet to take her eyes off Carrie. If she was going to die, she wanted the other woman to know she'd meant every word she'd said about her fate.

Carrie was doing everything possible to ignore Rachel. There were undercurrents in the room that Rachel didn't understand. Carrie was watching the two men who stood at Angelo's back and trying to relay some unspoken communication to them. They looked like exactly what they were. Hired thugs. Their suits were boxy and their minds empty except for whatever orders were tossed their way, and Carrie's frustration was growing palpable.

Angelo didn't like being ignored. "Now, tell me niece, who did this to your pretty face?"

Rachel didn't answer. She just kept her glare on Carrie.

"Ahh," Angelo said. "I believe I can connect the dots." He turned around and faced Carrie, and she stood defiantly in front of him.

"Has the money been transferred?" she asked.

"Yes. And I even added the extra hundred thousand you demanded to bring me Rachel alive. Though it wasn't in good form to mark her like this. She won't last nearly as long now."

"I did what I had to do," she said shrugging. She pulled out the envelope from the inside of her jacket and handed it over to Angelo. "And here's the list as requested. For no extra charge."

Angelo pulled out the list and scanned it before folding it and putting it in the inside pocket of his suit jacket. "I assume your travelling companions have been taken care of as well?"

"Yes. You could say they had an unfortunate accident," Carrie said, smirking in Rachel's direction. "Now, if you'll give me a minute to call and make sure the funds have been transferred into my account, I'll be on my way. Not that I don't believe you about the money," she said. "But I make it a point to never trust anyone."

Carrie walked over to the two guards as if she were going to tell them something, but the words never made it out of her mouth. Angelo moved with a speed not many people knew him capable of. The buck knife he habitually carried in a sheath at the small of his back was in his hand in a matter of seconds, and the lights from the hotel across the street flashed across the six inch silver blade.

Angelo grabbed Carrie by the hair and held the knife to her throat. Her hand automatically went to the holster at her side, but Angelo pressed harder with the blade until Rachel could see the thin line of blood dripping from the tip of the knife. Carrie dropped her hands.

"Do something, you fools," she called out to the two guards. "Kill him."

The men stood still and looked straight ahead, ignoring her pleas.

"Did you really think I wouldn't know about you bribing my men to turn against me?" Angelo asked. "You thought you were so clever, didn't you? Didn't you?" he demanded.

"Y-y-yes," Carrie stuttered.

"You know nothing of inspiring loyalty. Money is not the only motivator a person has. Do you think those men are more afraid of you than they are of me?" he whispered, running the blade of the knife down the side of her cheek.

Carrie's eyes were wide with fear and with the knowledge she'd gone too far.

"P-p-please," she begged. "I didn't mean it."

"I'd enjoy torturing you, but I just can't waste the time," Angelo said. He jerked back hard on her hair and sliced the knife across her throat. A spray of blood arced through the air and Angelo stepped back to avoid the sticky substance from getting on his clothes. He let Carrie fall to the ground and stepped over her body. He held the knife up in front of Rachel—the knife still coated with the blood of a woman she'd promised would die.

Rachel felt no sorrow in the death of Carrie. But she felt fear as her own death stared her in the face.

There was a pool on the roof of the Hancock Hotel. The way it glowed an eerie bluish green would be one of the things that would stay in his mind forever.

Shane didn't have a problem gaining access to the roof in the middle of the night. It had actually been rather simple. He'd showered the dust and blood from his face and body and changed into clothes that hadn't looked like they'd just been in an explosion. Cutter had made sure he was outfitted with a change of clothes and the weapon of his choice—plus any other materials he might need. They'd all been concealed easily inside a suitcase.

He'd checked into the hotel using Cutter's identification, since they looked the most alike physically, and checking in under Shane's own name would get him arrested as soon as they entered his information into the computer. He paid cash for the room and requested one of the upper floors. The bored desk clerk barely gave him a second glance as he signed Cutter's name to the receipt and she handed him the key card.

Shane rode the elevator up to seventeen. When the doors opened, he got off on his floor but walked past his room to the stairs at the end of the long hallway. He climbed the remaining three stories up and used his key card to access the roof level.

The wind and rain was frigid and pelted his face when he opened the door. The door shut behind him, and he took out the cell phone Dixon had given him out of his pocket. Dixon had the phone rigged so that one swipe across the electronic key slot would make the door unusable to anyone else. He'd have the whole rooftop to himself, not that anyone else would be crazy enough to be on the roof in the miserable weather besides him.

In the hotter months of the year, swimming or relaxing on the roof with the cool breeze would probably bring much needed relief to the body, but right now it was pure misery. The wind and other elements were always a factor when setting up for a shot, and he'd have to be careful not to overcompensate. He'd only have one chance.

Shane dropped the suitcase he was carrying onto the ground near the edge of the roof and unzipped it. He pulled a pair of night goggles over his eyes but then immediately tossed them aside. The lights from the hotel were too bright for them to do him any good. He'd have to rely on a pair of high powered binoculars and his scope. It was still a good ways off till dawn, so he didn't have to worry about that factor.

Shane set up the tripod for his rifle with quick, easy movements. The motions were as familiar to him as putting on his clothes every morning. Maybe more. He hunkered down on the cold roof and ignored the wet seeping into his clothes. His only concern was the job at hand.

His friends were twenty stories below, waiting on his signal before they infiltrated the building. He knew the four of them would do exactly what they'd set out to and get rid of all the threats that lurked in the building, but Rachel's safety would rely solely on him.

He used the binoculars and started on the lower floors of the building across the street. Angelo's goons were scattered around the entrances on the lower levels of the building and near the elevators. These guys were lower level security at best. None of them were very alert at this time of night. He saw a couple of them dozing in straight back chairs or on the floor against the walls. That would just make Alpha Squadron's job that much easier.

Rachel hadn't come into his sights yet, but he hadn't expected her to. According to Dixon's research, she'd be on one of the top floors. And Dixon was never wrong. Shane moved the binoculars up floor by floor until he came to the top level. If it weren't for the binoculars he never would have been able to see inside. The glass had already been tinted dark in preparation for the apartment that was being constructed inside.

And what he saw inside the room sickened him. Rachel was bound to a chair and her face was swollen and bloody. He could only see her in profile, but she was looking Angelo straight in the eyes as he talked to her, never backing down. There were two men at Angelo's back, and Shane could tell by the way the stood that they were much more dangerous than the men positioned on the bottom floors. There was a body on the floor that looked like Carrie, but he couldn't be a hundred percent sure. At least Angelo had taken that task out of his hands.

Shane used the cell phone Dixon had given him to signal that he'd found Rachel, and that the rest of the team could enter the building when ready. He couldn't worry about what they were doing or if they were walking into a trap. He could only focus on Rachel and the man who wanted her dead.

Shane breathed slowly through his mouth and slowed his heartbeat before looking through the scope on his rifle and placing his finger on the trigger. Thoughts of what had happened two years ago flooded his brain with the images of horror he saw in his dreams every night, and he cursed as he pulled away from the scope and laid flat on his back on the ground.

He had to get it together. This was a completely different circumstance, and Rachel wasn't Maggie. The cold rain beat down on his face, but his body temperature was hot. His pulse jumped in his neck and his thoughts were scattered. He closed his eyes and did a few breathing exercises, and then he crawled back into position and looked through the scope once again.

From what he could see, it looked like Angelo's rage was escalating, and Shane knew he could wait no longer.

For the first time in his life Shane's finger shook as he placed it on the trigger.

"Do you know why I wanted you brought here to me?" Angelo asked Rachel.

"Because you're insane," she said. She would have smiled just to piss him off, but the movement would have hurt too much.

"You always did have a smart mouth. Your father didn't discipline you nearly enough in my opinion."

"Leave my father out of this. In your wildest

dreams you'll never come close to being half the man he is."

"Don't you mean was?" Angelo asked with a Cheshire cat smile. He pulled the handkerchief out of his jacket pocket and wiped down the blade in his hand.

Rachel felt the color drain from her face and she became nauseated. She'd waited all this time and had never known the truth about what had happened to her father. She thought she'd prepared herself for the worst, but she'd sorely miscalculated.

Angelo flipped the knife in his hand and kept his eyes steady on hers. "Come now, Rachel. Don't disappoint me. Aren't you going to ask what happened to him? Aren't you the least bit curious to know how he died?"

Rachel bit the inside of her cheek to keep herself from screaming out loud. NO! she wanted to yell. She didn't want to know what had happened to her father. But the reasonable side of her brain told her she needed the closure. Needed to be able to finally lay her father to rest.

"What did you do to him?" she finally asked.

Angelo smiled at her and continued tossing his knife in the air, end over end, so Rachel was almost hypnotized by the motion.

"I paid Carrie to bring me Dom and the original

list that he'd handed over to Agent Culver. She brought me Dom as I'd asked, but unfortunately the list was nowhere to be found. No one seems to know what happened to it, but I have my own theories. Carrie was a greedy young woman, and she probably thought having her own copy might come in useful at some point. I couldn't blame her really. It's exactly why I wanted the list for myself. I let the transgression slide because I still had need of her inside the FBI. It's not as easy to bribe law enforcement as it used to be, and Carrie did have her uses."

Angelo tossed his knife to the other hand, and Rachel noticed the guards at Angelo's back were beginning to get antsy. Maybe they weren't as comfortable with a sociopathic boss as they liked to think.

"I'm on the list, you know," Angelo said. "Imagine how you'd feel if your own brother was going to turn you in. I couldn't let it happen, and the other families agreed with me. Everyone was so sad to get rid of Dom," he spat.

Anger flooded Angelo's face and he continued to toss the knife, round and round, only he hadn't noticed how tight he was gripping the blade each time he caught it. Blood dripped steadily down his wrist and onto the floor. "Everyone loved Dom like he was Santa Claus. People aren't afraid of Santa Claus. He was ruining us all."

Rachel jerked against the cuffs around her wrists, but found they were cinched tight. Angelo was losing control quickly and she'd already decided she wasn't going to go down easy. She wouldn't just sit quietly and wait for him to slice her throat. It just wasn't in her nature.

"Dom was a pathetic excuse for a man. I brought him to this very building and sat him just as you are now. I didn't give him the easy way out like I did with your friend here," he said, pushing Carrie's body over with the tip of his shoe so her gaping throat was exposed. "He didn't even have the decency to take it like a man when I started to work on him. He begged and pleaded the whole time, crying like a little girl, for me to stay away from you. I, of course, would have been glad to accommodate a dying man's last wishes, but then I found out he'd sent you a little surprise in the mail. I can admit I got a little overzealous with your father. He didn't last nearly as long as I'd have liked him to. Sometimes I forget my own strength and cut a little too deep."

Angelo looked down at his hand and noticed the blood for the first time. "See what I mean," he said, holding his palm up for her to see.

The guards at Dom's back were moving towards the elevator, each of them talking on their headsets, repeating the same command for each station to check in. Angelo didn't notice. He was in his own world.

Rachel wiggled her ankles and tried desperately to loosen the rope at her feet. She'd stopped watching the flipping knife and her gaze followed the two guards around the room. They pressed the button for the elevator, but it never arrived, so they split up and went to each side of the floor were the emergency exit stairs were located.

A hard slap brought Rachel's attention back to Angelo, bringing a moan of pain to her lips. He'd hit the same cheek as Carrie had earlier and blood dribbled down her chin. She breathed through her nose to fight the nausea and couldn't find the strength to groan when Angelo yanked her up by the hair so she was looking him in the face.

"I haven't finished my story yet," he said. "You're being very rude. Now, where was I?"

Rachel didn't make the mistake of taking her eyes off him again.

"Oh, yes. I had just killed your father. It's a moment I'll always remember. And now I have you in exactly the same spot. Ironic, isn't it?"

"What did you do with him?" Rachel was barely able to get the question out. Her face was swollen to the point where her mouth would only open so far and talking was difficult.

"What did I do with him?" Angelo laughed. "I'm not completely heartless. He was my brother after all. I gave him a decent burial. Last spring I had the most beautiful crop of roses bloom in my gardens. I like to think it's because Dom is such good fertilizer."

Tears coursed down Rachel's cheeks and she could tell her uncle was finished grandstanding. The end had come, and her only thought was that she'd never gotten to tell Shane she loved him. Now it was too late for both of them.

"Are you ready, Rachel?" he asked softly. "I'll try not to make it over too soon." The knife was back in his hand in the blink of an eye, but the chaos at the stairwell finally got his attention. Four men dressed in black, with their faces painted to match, burst through the doors. Rachel recognized Jax and the tears started falling faster. The fighting at the stairs was intense, and the guards put up a struggle that would have evened things up considerably if the numbers had been the same.

Angelo didn't waste time trying to save the lives of his bodyguards. He moved slowly behind Rachel and took her by the hair.

The guards were both face down on the floor and the four men in black were the only ones left standing. They each had their weapons pointed to the ground so as not to put Rachel in the line of fire.

"Congratulations, gentlemen. You've found me. But I won't be taken down alone. She'll die one way or the other."

The blade of the knife bit into her skin and she

held back a whimper of pain. She closed her eyes tightly and thought of Shane—about the last night they'd spent together and the lifetime they'd never get to see.

Glass shattered from across the room and she was left with no time to react. One minute she was praying for a quick death and the next her killer was laying crumpled on the ground behind her. She was frozen in shock, and the reality of what had happened didn't begin to set in until Jax came over and began to untie her.

"Oh, God," she wept. "Shane?" She grabbed Jax's arm as soon as her hands were free. "He's still alive?"

"Alive and well," he assured her. "But I'd give him another couple of minutes before he makes it over here. He's not as young as he used to be."

Rachel laughed through her tears. "I need to see him. Don't let anyone take me away until I see him."

"He'd kill me if I tried," Jax said. "No offense, honey, but you're not looking so good right now. Maybe you could make your reunion a quick one so we can get you to the hospital."

"Ambulance is on its way," one of the other men called out. "Along with the FBI. Should be an entertaining couple of hours."

As soon as the bullet left his rifle, Shane knew he'd made a direct hit. He barely took the time to disassemble his rifle and put it back in the suitcase before he was running back into the hotel. He rode the twenty floors down with agonizing impatience and ignored the stares of the desk clerks as he ran through the lobby and out the doors.

Traffic was light outside and he ran across Michigan Avenue, dodging taxis and other vehicles until he stood in front of Angelo Valentine's high-rise. He barely noticed the bodies that littered the floor on the inside or how smoothly the elevator ran as he rode his way to the top. All he could think about was Rachel. She was alive. And if she'd have him he'd make sure she stayed safe for the rest of his life.

The elevator doors opened and he ran onto the floor he'd just minutes before been looking at through his scope. He ignored the congratulations from his team members and searched for Rachel. She was sitting on the floor with her back against the wall and Cutter was looking over her bruises.

Suddenly he found himself unsure what to do. How to react. But then Rachel opened her eyes and looked straight at him as if she'd sensed him there all along. She held out her hand to him and he knew exactly where he belonged. Beside her. Forever.

Shane went to her and the sight of her beautiful face, so swollen and battered, made his knees weak and his trigger finger itch to kill the bastard one more time.

"Oh, baby," he said, taking her hand. He didn't know where else to touch her that wouldn't cause her pain.

"I'm okay," she said. "I thought you were dead." Fat tears gathered at the corner of her eyes and rolled down her cheeks. "I was so afraid, but when I thought I was going to die you were the only thing I could think of. And then you saved me."

"Ssh," Shane said. "Try not to talk. I know it hurts."

She nodded at him. Shane heard the stretcher being wheeled off the elevator and knew his time alone with her was short. He took a breath and prayed she'd understand what she meant to him. "It was you, Rachel, that saved me," he finally said. "I'm not whole without you, and you've managed to do something I thought was impossible."

"What's that?" she asked.

"You've chased the nightmares away. Love has that ability." He didn't move as the medics came and kneeled beside them. He had one last thing to say. "I love you, Rachel Valentine."

EPILOGUE

Rachel Valentine was a new woman.

Her dark hair was shorter now, a shiny cap that framed her face, making her eyes seem impossibly large and her cheekbones more prominent. Looking in the mirror every morning still gave her system a jolt, but she knew she would adjust as time passed.

With her new hair had come a new name, a new past, a new position at the community library, and a little white house with three bedrooms and a rose garden in Bakersfield, Indiana. She'd at first thought being so removed from the city would drive her crazy, but she was starting to think maybe she really was a small town girl at heart.

The important thing was that she was still alive.

Entering the Witness Protection Program had been her only option after the FBI had taken possession of the list and started making arrests. There had been a small hope inside her that her father's acquaintances wouldn't blame her for turning them in, but the hope she'd harbored had quickly been destroyed. Rachel had suffered a broken jaw and countless bruises thanks to Carrie, and she hadn't been out of the hospital a day before the first attempt was made on her life. If Shane hadn't been there to push her out of the way of the speeding delivery van, the mob contract that had been put out on her would have been easily fulfilled.

Rachel knelt in the grass in front of the small flower garden she'd planted in front of her new home and pulled weeds mindlessly while her thoughts wondered. Her driver's license might claim she was Karen Smith, and two years might have been added to her twenty-six, but she would always be Rachel Valentine on the inside. It was important for her to remember who she was. Where she came from.

Rachel told herself every morning that the sacrifices she'd made were all worth it. She wasn't a selfish person by nature, so she understood that anyone who was involved in her life—friends and lovers alike—would always be in danger as long as she remained a Valentine.

But God, how she missed Shane. There was an emptiness inside her that only he could fill. It had been months since she'd last seen him, and even then it had only been in passing as they'd both been swept away by FBI agents to give separate statements. The man in charge of the Witness Protection Program had thought it best she get established in her new life as quickly as possible, so she hadn't even been able to say goodbye to Shane or tell him she loved him one last time. Not saying goodbye was something she'd always regret.

The sound of gravel crunching under tires made her pulse quicken, but she brought her head up slowly and watched as a white pickup truck pulled into her driveway. The fear that someone would find her hadn't lessened over the months she'd lived with her new identity. She couldn't imagine it ever would.

Rachel stayed kneeling in the grass, but her hand grabbed the small .22 revolver she habitually carried in her pocket. She placed it on the ground beside her and waited patiently, prepared for whatever might happen. The sun was shining brightly and kept her from seeing her visitor clearly, so she brought her hand up to shade her eyes and watched as a large man got out of the truck.

"Oh, my God," she whispered and started to stand, but her knees gave way and her heart continued to hammer in her chest.

Long, deliberate strides headed in her direction and she forgot all about the revolver within her grasp. Denim clad legs knelt in the grass beside her, and a shiny, silver Sheriff's badge was passed briefly in front of her face.

"Maam? Are you all right?"

Rachel's expression turned to one of confusion as she looked at the badge again and then slowly brought her gaze up to look into a pair of familiar dark eyes.

"What? How?" she asked, dazed.

"The name's Quincy Ford. I'm the new Sheriff in Bakersfield. I was just driving through town and saw you as I passed by. I knew immediately that I had to stop and find out who the beautiful woman tending her roses was. And then I thought since I'm new in town that maybe we could grab some dinner, or make love or spend the rest of our lives together. In no particular order."

Rachel's breath caught on a sob and she threw herself into Shane's arms, kissing him with months worth of pent up passion and taking them both to the ground. She shuddered as his lips devoured hers and moaned as he ran his hands over her body. She became greedy in her wants and forgot where they were. Who they were. Only that they were together at last.

"Maybe we should take this inside, Sugar. I'd hate to have to arrest myself for public indecency."

Rachel choked out a watery laugh and reluctantly loosened her grip. Her face heated when Shane stood up and she saw his shirt was completely unbuttoned and his hair was sexily mussed. She took the hand he offered her and they walked into the house, thankful that none of her neighbors had witnessed her temporary insanity.

"I don't understand any of this," Rachel said, leaning against the kitchen counter. Shane sat down at the kitchen table, but she was too restless to mirror him, afraid if she took her eyes off him he'd suddenly be gone. "What are you doing here? How did you find me? What about your business? Your life?"

"I told you to trust me, Sugar. I've still got plenty of connections, and I decided I'd much rather be with you than alone in New Orleans. You are my life. I wanted to be here sooner, but there were a few details that had to be seen to first."

Rachel noticed the shadow that came over Shane's face and wondered what she'd missed over the last few months. "Can you talk about it?" she asked.

"I decided to put Jones in charge of my business and signed everything over to him. He's in bad shape. I barely recognized the man, and I've known him most of my life. He's harder, tougher, if that's even possible, and you can practically see the violence simmering under his skin. There's no more humor or sarcasm, and I can't really say I blame him.

I've been where he is, and nothing but time can make things better."

Shane rubbed a hand through his hair in frustration. "Jones spent more than a month in the hospital recovering from the bullet wound in his chest, and the day he was released from the hospital, the FBI decided he was the one they were going to hold accountable for this whole mess, not Director Shaw, as it should have been. The public and the media wanted a scapegoat, and he was the only one available who wasn't there to defend himself. The man's a war hero, and his entire career has been reduced to less than nothing."

"What did he do?"

"There was nothing he could do. Nothing I said in my testimony made any difference. They'd already made up their minds. Jones is acting like nothing's wrong, like it's just business as usual, but I know him too well. The country he's almost died for on more than one occasion has betrayed him, and I'm not sure it's a wound that can be healed."

Rachel didn't bother to mention that the wound Carrie had dealt to Jones's heart might be even harder to heal.

"I handed my agency over to him without giving him a lot of say in the matter," Shane said. "It was all I could do for him. All he'd let me do. He's not ready to face things yet. The rest of the team will check on him from time to time, and he knows my place now is here with you."

"And now you're the new Sheriff of Bakersfield," Rachel said, shaking her head.

Shane nodded. "And you're the new librarian who's giving the city council headaches with all your new ideas. I've already been warned about you. Part of the reason it took me so long to get here was I was waiting for the old Sheriff to retire. My former director at the Washington FBI office pulled a few strings to make sure the job was mine."

"And are the sheriff and librarian going to live happily ever after?"

Shane dug around in his pocket and pulled out a little black box, flipping open the lid and setting it on the table. The sight of it was enough to make her sit down across from him. The diamond inside and what it signified brought a sense of rightness over her. Contentment. The horrors of her past were going to be replaced with a future—a future filled with happiness and love and family.

"We've been through a lot together," Shane said. "We've come close to death and saved each other, in more ways than one. I love you, and I can't live the rest of my life without you. Will you marry me?"

"Yes," she said, and smiled as he slipped it onto her finger. "And I also remember you mentioning something about eating dinner and making love. In no particular order."

"We should definitely eat dinner later. I'm assuming you have a bed in this place," he said, pushing his chair back and coming to stand in front of her. Rachel squealed as he scooped her out of the chair and into his arms, and her heart flipped in her chest as she saw the heat in his eyes.

"I've been waiting a long time to make love to you again," Shane said, "so I hope you don't have any plans for the next three or four days."

"We do need the practice in calling out each others new names," Rachel said thoughtfully. She nipped his ear with her teeth, and took pleasure in his indrawn breath and the way her touch made him stumble as he hurried to get to her bedroom. "But I have to go to work at some point. The city council might get suspicious and start snooping around to see where I am."

Shane laid her down on the bed and kissed her softly—reverently—memorizing the feel of her lips against his. "I'm the Sheriff," he finally said as he broke off the kiss. "I'll put in a good word for you."

She laughed and opened her arms to him, accepting the weight of his body on hers. "My hero," she said.

ABOUT THE AUTHOR

Liliana Hart is the pseudonym for an author of more than a dozen books. She's a workaholic and doesn't get to do near as much exciting stuff as her characters because she's too busy writing their stories. She lives in Texas with her husband and cats, and loves to be contacted by readers.

Connect with me online:
www.lilianahart.com
http://twitter.com/Liliana_Hart
http://facebook.com/LilianaHart

38472933R00146

Made in the USA
Lexington, KY
10 January 2015